"Champagne?"

"I thought it was a good idea, just to mark the occasion."

"What occasion?" asked Olivia.

Max looked at her with unnerving directness, no trace of smile softening the hardness of his features. "You're a beautiful, intelligent woman, Olivia, and I've enjoyed your company today. But tomorrow I'm probably going to make your little sister very unhappy, and when that happens I don't hold out much hope of any further social contact where you and I are concerned. So tonight is special, a one-off deserving of vintage champagne as an overture to an evening spent with a very special lady I wish I'd met in very different circumstances." He raised his glass in toast. "To your beautiful green eyes...."

Dear Reader,

Those who dare to dream reap rich rewards, because sometimes daydreams really do come true.

All my adult life I yearned to see Venice, and at last, not long ago, the dream became reality. We cruised down the Grand Canal past ancient, exquisite buildings gilded with sunlight, drank espressos among the pigeons on the Piazza San Marco and lunched at the fabled Harry's Bar. Venice lived up to all expectations as we crossed picturesque bridges over narrow, glittering canals to explore the city they called the Queen of the Adriatic. So surrender to the unique allure of Venice and Italy as you read *A Brief Encounter*, and share in one of my personal dreams come true.

Sincerely,

Catherine George

A BRIEF
ENCOUNTER
Catherine George

Harlequin Books

TORONTO • NEW YORK • LONDON
AMSTERDAM • PARIS • SYDNEY • HAMBURG
STOCKHOLM • ATHENS • TOKYO • MILAN
MADRID • WARSAW • BUDAPEST • AUCKLAND

ISBN 0-373-03360-5

A BRIEF ENCOUNTER

CHAPTER ONE

THE entrance hall of the Villa Bellagio was a high-ceilinged room with thin rugs on gleaming wood floors, exquisite wall frescoes and chandeliers like great bouquets of fragile blossom fashioned from Venetian glass. Silver-framed photographs of distinguished visitors to the hotel stood on a grand piano in the corner, old, fragile porcelain gleamed from glass cases, and sunshine warm and gold as honey poured through glass doors open to a shady garden where a swimming pool glittered like a jewel in its setting of sheltering evergreens.

But the most recent arrival at the hotel had no eyes for the beauty of her surroundings. She stared at the receptionist in disbelief.

'My sister isn't here?'

'I regret not, *signora*.' The receptionist smiled a little uneasily, and handed over a letter from one of the pigeonholes on the wall behind her. 'Sophie left this for you, Miss Maitland. When you have read it the porter will escort you to your room.'

Olivia opened the letter with foreboding, cold dismay hidden behind her large sunglasses as she read Sophie's familiar scrawl.

Darling Liv, don't be angry with me for standing you up. It's only for a day or two until you get to Pordenone. I had the chance of a little holiday with my friend Andrea so I grabbed it. I know it means leaving you on your own for a day or two until you get to the Villa Nerone, but you do things like that all the time in your work anyway, and I've given strict instructions to everyone at the Bellagio to look after you, arrange a trip to Venice—anything you want. So till Saturday, *ciao, cara*, lots of love, Sophie.

Olivia put the note away, managed a smile for the handsome young man waiting with her luggage, then followed him from the hall through the open doors, skirting the garden and the pool as they made for a colonnade with stone arches open to the garden on one side, a two-storey row of bedrooms on the other. Sophie's absence had come as such a shock that Olivia felt suddenly weary as she climbed a flight of smooth stone steps to the upper floor. The porter ushered her into a large, pretty bedroom with a view of the pool from its trio of windows, told her tea was available at one of the tables on the terrace, then smiled with pleasure in response to her generous tip. Olivia closed the door behind him, stared abstractedly at the delightful vista of pool and gardens for a moment or two, then told herself to snap out of it. Sophie was no longer a child. And from her letter she was obviously well and happy, and would be in Pordenone in less than forty-eight hours. So for the time being the obvious thing was to get on with the job and note down first impressions of the Villa Bellagio.

In her capacity as a senior tour consultant for a specialist travel agency, Olivia was on an expenses-paid research trip to three hotels in Northern Italy. This afternoon she'd arrived at Marco Polo airport in Venice, picked up the car hired in advance from

London, and driven from Venice on the Treviso road to make her first stop at the Villa Bellagio, where her sister was working as a receptionist during her summer vacation from university. Sophie was reading French and Italian, and had suggested the Bellagio to Olivia as perfect for the discerning traveller, as well as for a little get together for the two sisters. Too bad one of us preferred to take off with someone else instead, thought Olivia wryly.

Postponing notes and unpacking, Olivia brushed her glossy short hair into shape, decided both her face and her crisp cotton shirt and skirt would do, and left her room to go in search of tea. This was served on the terrace under a striped umbrella at a table with a pink linen cloth and thin china, where she was provided with pots of hot water, slices of lemon and a supply of teabags of flavours varying from English breakfast to the lesser known delights of strawberry and jasmine.

In the warm afternoon sunshine, with the happy shouts of children splashing in the pool under the eyes of their lazing elders, Olivia began to unwind as she sipped her tea, the shock of Sophie's absence gradually receding. She was alone at the small cluster of tables, at a time when most people would be changing for dinner, or still sunbathing round the pool. Her professional concentration reasserted itself as she took note of the statues and the great stone urns filled with hydrangeas like great globes of coral against the blinding white gravel of the terrace. Sophie was right, she decided. Villa Bellagio was a very beautiful place. And now she was more in command of herself it was time to do her job and begin her report on it.

Olivia refused offers of more tea from the hovering waiters and went for a stroll round the pool, smiling as she watched a trio of tanned, excited children splashing each other under the indulgent gaze of their parents. Although it was early evening by this time, the sun was still hot, and Olivia gave in to temptation and stretched out on one of the steamer chairs, fatigued more by worry about Sophie's absence than the journey from London. The Alitalia flight had been swift and punctual, with breathtaking glimpses of glittering waterways and gilded domes as they descended towards Venice. Nor had the drive to the Bellagio presented any problems, thanks to Sophie's clear directions. In fact, Olivia thought, as she got up to make for her room, normally she would be full of energy at this point. But it was useless to worry any more about Sophie. Nothing could be done until their Saturday rendezvous at the Villa Nerone, the next stop on Olivia's fact-finding mission.

When she returned to her room Olivia took out her notebook and recorded her impressions on the décor, which was simple but charming, with louvred shutters at the windows and plain blue covers on the beds, which, like the rest of the furniture were reproductions of eighteenth-century design. No air-conditioning, she noted, but an electronic anti-mosquito device was provided, and the pretty little bathroom was generously supplied with towels and all the shampoos and gels and shoe-cleaning sachets the modern traveller expected. Despite its general air of antiquity the hotel was scrupulously clean and well-kept, Olivia noted in approval; also the lamps worked and there was a small, well-stocked refrigerator disguised as a cabinet. Olivia wrote a few words of praise in the comments section of the page, and put her book away in favour of a long soak in the bath.

She was just emerging from it, swathed in towels, when the telephone rang. She raced to pick it up, then slumped down on the bed in relief at the sound of her sister's voice.

'Liv? It's me——'

'Sophie, thank heavens! Where on earth *are* you?'

'In Florence! Isn't it a fantastic place? You always made me so envious about it, and now I've seen it for myself—the statue of David's just as incredible——'

'Never mind David,' broke in Olivia sternly. 'Why didn't you let me know before I left?'

'Oh, Liv, don't be cross! You were coming anyway, and this all happened a bit suddenly, so I had the time coming to me, and I'll be seeing you in a couple of days, so I jumped at the chance. Don't worry. I'm fine. And I'm not alone.'

'Who *is* this company of yours, Sophie?'

'You'll find out on Saturday—Andrea's very keen to meet you. By the way, I'm staying with Andrea's family tonight, so no need to fret. I've told everyone at the hotel to treat you like a queen, and make sure you have everything you want. No marauding males will accost you, I promise—unless you want one to! Oops, there's my money gone. *Ciao*——'

And before Olivia could ask any more questions the line went dead. She put down the phone slowly, not nearly as reassured by Sophie's call as hoped. Her little sister, she thought, eyes narrowed, was up to something. But until it was possible to find out what, exactly, the only sensible plan was to enjoy some of the Bellagio's famed cuisine, have an early night and

a good sleep, and spend tomorrow in her long an-
ticipated exploration of Venice.

Olivia dried and brushed her leaf-brown hair into
the cleverly cut layers which framed her face, then
applied a minimum of make-up with practised speed.
Used to dining alone in strange hotels, she wore her
usual type of clothes, a pine-green silk shirt with a
tailored cream linen suit, and tonight, with the excuse
that her eyes felt dry and full of sand after her intense
concentration on the drive from Venice, she added
her dark glasses to counteract an unwelcome feeling
of vulnerability.

This was partly dispelled by her welcome to the
dining-room. The head waiter, who introduced himself
as Carlo, ushered her to a corner table, where he drew
out a chair facing the floodlit garden before handing
her a large menu. He clicked his fingers and instantly
a young waiter arrived with grissini, the crisp bread
sticks Olivia adored, plus a basket of rolls, a dish of
butter and some San Pellegrino water for her to sip
while she made her choice. Carlo withdrew to let her
weigh up the delights of scallops in the chef's special
sauce or a plain tomato and mozzarella salad to begin,
and when Olivia looked up from her menu she found
the tables were filling rapidly, mainly with families
and couples, some of whom greeted her pleasantly as
they took their places.

She chose the salad as prelude to Carlo's rec-
ommendation of a mixed grill of fish, which was quite
superb, with sole, turbot, scampi and scallops as the
main attraction. The fish arrived sizzling at the table
in its own pan, to be filleted and served by Carlo
himself, and Olivia ate with enjoyment, taking mental
notes of the simple, exquisitely prepared food, though

disappointing the waiter by her refusal of a pudding. She elected to drink her coffee at the table, preferring to remain gazing at the stars and the floodlit garden rather than venture alone into the bar. She sipped slowly, savouring the sound of animated multilingual conversation around her, then after a while, early though it was, decided she had no alternative but to go to bed.

Olivia paused to look at some antique jewellery displayed in a glass case then looked up involuntarily as a man with a hard, sunburned face, and black curling hair in dire need of a barber, strode through the entrance doors to be greeted by the manager himself at the reception desk. The newcomer towered over Signor Ferrante, firing low-toned urgent questions which the man answered by spreading his hands in wry apology as he leaned up to mutter confidentially in the newcomer's ear. Instantly the man swung round to stare at Olivia.

She turned on her heel, head in the air, and made for the double doors which led to the colonnade, but before she could reach them the manager hurried to intercept her.

'Signora Maitland, I am Enrico Ferrante, the manager of the Villa Bellagio. I trust you enjoyed your dinner?'

Olivia inclined her head. 'I did, very much.'

'*Bene*. I am so glad.' He smiled politely, then gestured towards the man who leaned against the reception desk, watching them. 'Would you permit me to introduce you to another guest? Mr Hamilton is a countryman of yours and would be most grateful for a few words with you.'

Reluctant, but with no real reason to refuse, Olivia nodded graciously, but stayed very deliberately where she was, making the impatient-looking stranger cross the hall to speak to her.

'Miss Maitland, allow me to present Mr Max Hamilton.' The manager bowed, then withdrew with obvious relief.

'How do you do,' said the man brusquely.

Olivia inclined her head, waiting impassively for the 'few words' he was so anxious to have with her.

'It was your sister I really wanted to meet,' he said, looking down his nose at her in a way which raised every hackle Olivia possessed. She returned the look with hauteur, glad he couldn't hear the alarm bells ringing in her head.

'My sister?' she said glacially.

'Apparently she left last week on an unexpected trip,' went on her companion grimly. 'Which happens to be one hell of a coincidence.'

'I have no idea what you mean, Mr Hamilton,' said Olivia, incensed. 'Please explain yourself, and briefly, please. I've travelled here from London today and I'm tired.'

'I've travelled a hell of a sight farther than that,' returned the man without sympathy. 'After an SOS from my brother's fiancée I've come straight here from Qatar instead of going back to London as I intended.'

Olivia frowned in astonishment. 'What has all this to do with me?'

'Your sister's name is Sophie, and she has been working here as a receptionist this summer, I assume?'

'Yes,' she admitted reluctantly.

His lips tightened. 'My brother's missing, and it's highly probable your sister's gone off with him.'

'This is outrageous,' declared Olivia, bristling. 'What possible reason can you have for believing that?'

'They were seen leaving together. Besides, I'm told you expected to find her here when you arrived,' said Max Hamilton flatly, '*and* that her absence came as a shock to you.'

'I admit I expected to find her here, but my visit isn't just a holiday. I'm here on business, so Sophie's absence just means a slight change of plan. She's meeting me on Saturday instead.'

'Where?' pounced the man, bending towards her.

Olivia retreated a step. 'I fail to see what our plans have to do with you, Mr Hamilton. I don't know your brother, and neither does Sophie. You're very much mistaken. She's travelling with a girl called Andrea.'

Max Hamilton's smile set her teeth on edge. 'You got the sex wrong! Andrea's the name my brother was landed with at birth, only he prefers to answer to Drew. The stupid idiot's due to be married in two weeks' time, and his bride-to-be is getting pretty uptight about his absence. I've been sent to find him and bring him home.'

Olivia stared at him stonily from behind the dark lenses, her brain working at furious speed. If what this objectionable man said was true, no wonder Sophie hadn't let her get a word in during their telephone conversation. And she had a sinking feeling that it *was* the truth, and the reason why Sophie had been so cagey—and excited. Sophie was twenty years old, very pretty and very clever, but common sense wasn't always her strongest point.

At last Olivia shrugged coolly. 'Even if what you say is true and I had any intention of helping you, I can't, Mr Hamilton. I have no idea where Sophie is at this moment, only that she's meeting me on Saturday at the hotel which is my next port of call. Goodnight.' She turned away, but Max Hamilton caught her by the wrist.

'Wait!'

Olivia stared in such outrage that he dropped her hand like a hot coal.

'I'm sorry,' he said, with such an obvious fight to be conciliatory she felt a twinge of amusement. 'But surely you can appreciate what a hellish spot Drew's put me in!'

'I can, ideed,' said Olivia coldly. 'But I refuse to believe that your problem is anything to do with either my sister or myself.'

Max Hamilton glared blackly at her, then let out a weary sigh and rubbed a hand over his eyes. 'Look, Miss Maitland, could we have a quiet drink in the bar and talk this over?'

'What you really mean is, will I give you the exact time and place of my rendezvous with my sister on Saturday,' she retorted.

'You'd be doing Sarah a good turn if you did,' he said bleakly. 'It cut me up to have her crying her heart out on the line to Doha yesterday.'

'Sarah being the abandoned bride?' said Olivia, winning herself another black-browed scowl. 'Mr Hamilton, you have no proof that my sister is with your brother. But even if they are together it's unlikely Sophie knows about any wedding. If there's any leading astray involved, your brother's the culprit. How old is he?'

'Twenty-eight,' he said reluctantly.

Olivia's eyes kindled behind the dark lenses. 'Sophie is twenty,' she informed him scathingly. 'She's a student, earning some money by working through her vacation, and gaining experience in one of her languages while she's doing it. I'm the one entitled to be angry, Mr Hamilton, not you.'

He frowned. 'She's that young? Hell, Drew must be off his head. I suppose she's pretty?' he added, resigned.

Olivia nodded distantly. 'Yes, she is. Though I fail to see the relevance.'

'If Drew *has* taken off with your sister, Miss Maitland, she must be pretty. He tends to go for the package rather than the contents.'

She gave him a hostile look. 'Including his bride-to-be?'

The hard, bony face softened fractionally. 'Sarah's the exception. Which is why he's marrying her.'

Olivia breathed in deeply. '*If*, and I do mean *if* my sister is with your brother, one thing you can be very sure of: he hasn't said a word about a fiancée or a wedding. Sophie may be young, but she's neither brainless nor unscrupulous.'

Max Hamilton shrugged. 'I'm sure you're right. But when Drew wants something he can be bloody single-minded. In other words, if your sister's charms are potent enough he won't mention Sarah.'

'You paint a charming picture of him!'

'I'm a good few years his senior, and I'm very fond of him, but I don't see Drew through rose-tinted glasses, believe me.' Max Hamilton eyed a party of voluble guests arriving to collect their keys. 'Miss Maitland—please—just give me five minutes of your time over a drink in the bar. It's quieter there.' He saw her glance at her watch, and said quickly, 'it's not late.'

Olivia eyed him dubiously, thawing slightly as she noted the fatigue marks smudging his dark eyes, the lines of weariness in the strong, harsh-featured face. His linen suit was creased from travelling and he looked as though a night's sleep would have done more good than a drink.

'Oh, very well,' she said, with reluctance. 'But only for a few minutes.'

'Thank you.' Max Hamilton led her across the hall towards the sound of soft music played on a grand piano in a corner of another high-ceilinged, frescoed room worthy of a better description than mere bar. He seated Olivia on a sofa in a quiet corner farthest from the piano, then summoned a waiter.

Olivia asked for a plain tonic water, her companion for a cognac, and an awkward silence prevailed between them until the drinks arrived, then he drank deeply from his, set down the glass, and turned a morose look on Olivia.

'I apologise for any rudeness earlier. Diplomacy has never been my strong point.'

She nodded in pointed agreement as she sipped her drink.

His lips tightened. 'But since your sister and my brother left on the same day and were seen chatting together quite a lot while he was here, it's pretty obvious that they must be together. Particularly as her friend's name just happens to be Andrea.'

Olivia raised her head, glad of her dark glasses as she looked him in the eye. 'Mr Hamilton, I sympathise with your dilemma. But until I meet Sophie on Saturday and hear the truth from her I flatly refuse to believe she took off with someone she'd only just met. How long did your brother stay here at the hotel?'

'Two days,' said her companion grudgingly. 'In company with a cameraman and sound technician.'

Olivia's eyebrows rose. 'A little high-profile for conducting a clandestine romance! Did this entourage take off with the happy pair too?'

Max Hamilton's wide mouth tightened as he explained that his brother worked in television as a presenter for a motoring programme. In company with his crew, Drew Hamilton had been putting an AC Cobra open two-seater through its paces in the Pre-Alps, and had called in for a photo-session at the Villa Bellagio as a finale.

'Oh,' said Olivia heavily. 'He's *that* Drew Hamilton.'

The young man in question, lanky, blond and confident, with narrow laughing eyes and a wide white grin much in evidence as he roared around the country lanes in expensive cars, had rocketed the female viewing figures for the programme in question. If Drew Hamilton *had* made a set at her sister, Olivia had a sinking feeling that two days' acquaintance might well have been enough. With a trip to Florence thrown in, Sophie wouldn't have had the strength to refuse. Suddenly her eyes lit up.

'Wait a minute! Sophie can't be with your brother, Mr Hamilton. She said she was staying with Andrea's family tonight!'

To her surprise her companion looked grimmer than ever. 'Did she, now! Hell—the idiot must have taken her to stay with his mother in Sacile.'

'His mother?'

'He's my stepbrother. His mother is Italian, hence the name Andrea. Drew is the apple of her eye. If he wants to jilt Sarah two weeks before the wedding and take another girl home to Luisa she'll make no objection. Her baby boy can do no wrong.' His mouth twisted in a cynical smile, then he signalled to the waiter. 'I need another brandy before I can face a phone call to my stepmother. Can't I persuade you to something stronger?'

Olivia shook her head. 'Mr Hamilton, do you really believe your brother's taken a strange girl to stay at his mother's home on the very eve of his wedding to someone else?'

'I bloody well hope not,' he said savagely, then made a gesture of apology. 'Sorry. I haven't been in the company of women much for the past couple of months. My social graces are a tad rusty. I'll just fortify myself with this first, then go and ring Luisa.'

Olivia got up as he downed his drink. 'Will you ring my room to let me know what you find out? I'm in thirty-four.'

He jumped up, nodding. 'I'm only a few doors away. I'll be in touch as soon as I find anything out.'

They walked in constrained silence along the gleaming marble floor of the colonnade and up the worn stone steps to the upper storey. 'I'll expect to hear from you shortly, then,' she said stiffly, as they paused outside her door.

'Right.' He looked down at her as she opened it and switched on the light. 'I warn you, it may take some time. Luisa and I don't communicate easily.'

'Try using some tact!' advised Olivia tartly.

To her surprise he grinned, his teeth showing white against his deep-dyed tan in the subdued lighting. 'You mean improve on my approach to you earlier on?'

'Exactly.' She took off her dark glasses and smiled at him in return. 'You catch a lot more flies with honey.'

Max Hamilton's grin disappeared abruptly as he stared down at her in silence so prolonged Olivia felt uneasy. 'Does your sister look like you, Miss Maitland?' he asked at last.

'There's a certain resemblance, yes.'

He nodded slowly, his eyes moving over her face feature by feature. 'Not so hard to understand Drew, after all, then.' He gave her a mocking salute. 'I'll talk to you later.'

CHAPTER TWO

OLIVIA sat in a chair by the window, looking down on the floodlit garden in a state of tension as she waited for the phone to ring. The minutes ticked by with nerve-stretching slowness until a quiet knock on the door finally brought her to her feet.

'Who is it?' she asked sharply.

'Hamilton.'

Olivia threw open the door, staring up into the grim dark face impatiently. 'Well?' she flung at him.

'Could we take a turn in the garden?' he countered. 'It's a long story, and I need some air.'

Something about him quenched any thought of argument. Without a word Olivia locked her door and went down the stairs with him to walk among the statues and floodlit paths in front of the hotel. Max Hamilton waved her to a wrought-iron bench under a lamp, and sat down beside her.

'They're not in Sacile,' he said without preamble. 'Neither is my stepmother. She's in France on a visit to friends. After that she's going straight on to England for the wedding.'

Olivia let out the breath she'd been holding. 'How do you know?'

'I spoke to Daria, her housekeeper. The *signora*, she informed me, left last week, and will not be back for a month. Signor Andrea has not been to the house, nor has he telephoned, and although she's given me a number where I can reach Luisa in France Daria begged me not to do so unless vitally necessary. The *signora* will surely go mad with worry if she hears her beloved Andrea is missing. I am required to do all the worrying myself, and find him before the *signora* discovers he is missing,' he added caustically.

Olivia, who by this time wasn't sure exactly what she was worrying about most as regarded Sophie, eyed him with rather less hostility than before. 'You sound as though this is nothing new.'

'It isn't,' he assured her. 'I'm sorry I took so long, but after talking to Daria I rang Sarah, who still hasn't heard from Drew and is utterly convinced he's dead, or kidnapped, or anything other than merely missing believed skiving.'

'That's a bit cynical,' observed Olivia.

'Miss Maitland, I've knocked about the world quite a bit in the course of my job, and the one thing it's taught me above all else is that gullibility gets you nowhere.'

'What is your job?' she asked curiously.

'Engineering consultancy. I'm based in London, but I travel the world in a sort of trouble-shooting capacity, mainly to the Middle East and various parts of Africa.'

'Were you due back in the UK instead of coming to Italy?'

'Too damned right I was,' he said savagely. 'I've been in Qatar for a couple of months and could have done without the detour at this particular moment in time. Fortunately this was my father's favourite hotel. My family's well known here, which is why Rico Ferrante gave me his theory about your sister.'

'He had no right to,' snapped Olivia. 'The fact that she left the hotel the same day as your brother is probably pure coincidence.'

Max Hamilton stretched out his long legs wearily. 'Time will tell. Where are you meeting her?'

'The Villa Nerone——' Olivia bit her lip, glaring at him. 'Oh very neat, Mr Hamilton! I must be more tired than I thought.'

'That's near Pordenone,' he said swiftly.

'Is that significant?'

'So is Sacile.'

They stared at each other for a moment, then Olivia rose wearily to her feet.

'Time I went to my room, I think. Thank you for filling me in on the story so far, Mr Hamilton.'

He fell into step with her as they made for the colonnade. 'My name is Max,' he said, surprising her. 'Since we seem linked by fate—and our respective siblings—it seems silly to stay on formal terms.'

'It hardly matters,' she said distantly; 'we're unlikely to meet again.'

'I wouldn't count on that. Tell me your name,' he insisted.

'Olivia.'

He eyed her assessingly as they mounted the stone stairs together for the second time that night. 'It suits you.'

'I'm glad you think so.' She paused outside her door, hesitated, then held out her hand. 'Goodnight. I hope you track down your brother.'

'You're still convinced he's not with your sister?'

Olivia, who was very much afraid he was, nodded resolutely. 'Sophie's not the kind to succumb to a handsome stranger on such short acquaintance, believe me. Even a minor celebrity like your brother. Incidentally,' she added, suddenly frowning. 'If a television crew was with him at the hotel, what happened to them?'

'They arrived back on schedule, giving Sarah a message to the effect that Drew was following on alone later. She assumed he was visiting Luisa and didn't take much notice at first. Now she's panicking.' Max looked down at her questioningly. 'What will you do now?'

'Go on with my schedule. I haven't been to Venice before, so tomorrow I'll do some sightseeing there, come back here for the night, complete my report on the Bellagio then go on to Pordenone and the Villa Nerone in time to meet my sister at noon on Saturday,' said Olivia succinctly. 'I've now given you every scrap of information I possess, so I'll say goodnight.'

'Thank you, Olivia,' he said gravely. 'Try to get a good night's sleep. Or are you used to worrying about Sophie?'

'No,' she said stiffly. 'I'm not. She's a caring, responsible girl. Normally, anyway. I shall be very interested to discover what—or who—is responsible for this sudden impulse of hers. She's an adult, and entitled to do what she likes, of course, but she doesn't worry Father or me very much.'

'No mother?' asked Max quietly.

'She died when Sophie was ten. I was nineteen, so I took over the role after that. But I try not to overdo it. Goodnight.' Olivia smiled politely, and went into her room, locking the door behind her.

After a disturbed, restless night Olivia woke early to a beautiful day bright with sunshine. She took a

shower and dressed in a long green cotton skirt striped
in the cream of her thigh-length silk knit sweater.
Wearing flat beige canvas pumps and carrying a
matching holdall large enough to take her notebook
and camera and various odds and ends, Olivia went
down to breakfast to find that, early though she was,
Max Hamilton was already seated at the table she'd
dined at the night before. He got up quickly and held
out the chair beside him, giving her no option but to
join him.

'Good morning, Olivia, did you sleep well?'

She shook her head. 'No news, I suppose?'

He shook his head. 'Frankly I don't know what the
hell to do next.'

A waiter arrived to take their orders, and further
conversation was suspended until they were provided
with rolls and preserves and pots of fragrant coffee.

'I think you've made up your mind on that, if
you're honest,' observed Olivia eventually, buttering
a roll. 'You intend to be at the Villa Nerone at twelve
noon on Saturday to catch your brother with my little
sister and drag him home to his wedding by the scruff
of his neck.'

Max, who looked a different man this morning, in
a crisp short-sleeved shirt and khakis, gave her a faint,
crooked smile. 'Your opinion of me obviously hasn't
improved overnight. Though I don't see what else I
can do.'

'For starters a word in a few sympathetic ears round
here might help,' said Olivia. 'If I can find one who
speaks English I'm going to have a chat with one of
Sophie's colleagues, and see what I can find out.'

Max eyed her with dawning respect. 'Great idea. If you draw a blank I could talk with some of the waiters.'

Olivia smiled at him cajolingly. 'Mr Hamilton——'

'I thought we'd agreed on Max.'

'As you wish. Would you blow a fuse if I pointed out that it's easy to see you're a man used to giving orders rather than making tactful requests? In other words, would you let me have a shot at talking to the staff myself first?'

He turned the dark, unequivocal scrutiny on her, making her wish she'd worn her sunglasses. 'Would *you* blow a fuse,' he echoed mockingly, 'if I said that when you smile like that I doubt anyone refuses you anything?'

'Untrue,' she said shortly. 'My Italian is pretty basic as yet, so your assistance may well be needed. Though I'm not sure most of the staff here speak enough English to communicate. Anyway, I'll see what I can do once I've drunk this coffee. Until I've asked some questions I'll have no enthusiasm for sightseeing.'

'If you've never seen Venice before, you soon will have,' he assured her.

Olivia explained what she did for a living. 'Up to now I've specialised in Spain and Portugal, because I speak both those languages, but I've had Italy added to my patch so I've done a crash course in Italian for starters. I'll go on studying it when I get home.'

Max Hamilton drained his coffee-cup then raised a dark eyebrow in enquiry. 'Could I propose myself as guide for the day? I'm stuck with time on my hands until I get to Pordenone tomorrow. And you might learn more about Venice with a guide.'

Olivia eyed him doubtfully. 'You mean we keep to some kind of truce today before war breaks out tomorrow?'

'It doesn't have to be war! Once your sister learns the truth she'll probably send Drew packing, and presto, your problem is solved.'

'But not Sophie's,' retorted Olivia. '*If* she's with your stepbrother, something I'm by no means sure of, it must be because she's in love with him. Which means she'll be heartbroken when she learns the truth. It's not something I look forward to, believe me.'

His mouth twisted. 'You're obviously a lot better at relationships than I am.'

All animation drained from Olivia's face. 'Not really,' she said distantly, and got up. 'I'd better start asking questions.'

Max jumped to his feet. 'I'll get a newspaper and bag two chairs on the far side of the pool. Join me as soon as you can.'

'Giving orders again, Mr Hamilton?' she said tartly as they left the restaurant.

He shrugged. 'Old habits die hard. Would "please" turn it into a request?'

'Not exactly—but it's an improvement.'

A different receptionist was presiding at the desk, but to Olivia's relief the girl spoke very good English. Her name was Floria and she was perfectly willing to help the *signora*. But when Olivia began asking questions about Sophie Floria's eyes took on a guarded look even as she admitted she'd been present when Sophie left the Bellagio.

'Did she leave alone?' asked Olivia gently. 'Please tell me, Floria. It's very important.'

The girl cast a hunted look about the deserted reception hall. She bit her lip then gave a very Latin shrug. 'No, *signora,* she was not alone. She went with Signor Hamilton in his sports car. She—she was laughing, because the car is small and open and Signor Hamilton drives very fast. Sophie said she would be blown to pieces by the time she got to Venezia——'

'Venice?' pounced Olivia.

'*Si, signora*. From there she was going to Firenze.' Floria looked very unhappy. 'I hope you are not angry with her.'

Olivia managed a reassuring smile. 'No, of course not, and thank you, Floria, you've been very helpful. I'm seeing her tomorrow, so she'll be able to tell me all her adventures herself.'

Olivia walked very slowly out of the hall and into the garden as she digested the information, wishing she could keep it to herself. But Max Hamilton was sitting in one of a pair of steamer chairs drawn well away from the others, watching her as she approached.

'Any luck?' he asked, getting to his feet.

Olivia nodded reluctantly. 'Bullseye first time. Floria at Reception was very helpful. I don't think she was keen on confiding in me, but in the end she admitted that Sophie had been given a lift in your brother's car.'

'So they did leave together,' said Max brusquely.

'According to Floria, only to Venice.'

'Like hell it was,' said Max savagely. 'They've obviously gone off on a little jaunt in the Cobra together. I apologise for my brother, Olivia. He should have known a damn sight better.'

'I'm sure he didn't drag Sophie off by the hair,' said Olivia, trying to be fair. 'Though I still say she knows nothing about Sarah—and the wedding.'

They sat in brooding silence for a while, then Max turned to her questioningly. 'How were you proposing to get to Venice?'

'By car and *vaporetto*,' she said glumly.

'Hired car?'

'Yes, why?'

Max smiled faintly. 'I came by taxi from Marco Polo last night. If I'm going to act as your Venice guide you'll have to give me a lift.'

Olivia shrugged. 'Right. Not that I feel much enthusiasm for the trip at the moment.'

'One look at Venice will change your mind!'

Max Hamilton was right. After the short car journey, which Olivia found rather testing with a man like Max in the passenger seat watching her every move, it was a relief to get on the *vaporetto* in the warm, salt-scented sunshine. She stood in the open centre portion of the vessel as Max advised, to get the maximum view of the famous *palazzos* and buildings as they entered the Grand Canal.

'The astonishing thing,' gasped Olivia, 'is this strong sense of *déjà vu*. Venice has featured in so much cinema and television that I feel I've been here before!'

Max stood behind her, with a long brown hand on the rail beside her to keep her steady as she leaned out to a perilous degree in her eagerness not to miss anything. 'The Serenissima's certainly looking her best for you today. Sometimes it can be very overcast in Venice in July. Today it isn't even too hot.'

'It may not be to someone just returned from the desert,' she retorted, laughing up at him. 'To me it's quite hot enough, thank you. I wish I'd brought a hat.'

'I'll treat you to one from one of the stalls on the mole when we get to San Marco.' He smiled challengingly. 'If I buy you a hat will you take the glasses off?'

'Afraid not—they're prescription lenses. I need them to see. I'm short-sighted.'

'I'm almost relieved to hear there's a flaw in your perfection, Miss Maitland.'

Olivia was too engrossed in her surroundings to argue the point. Her eyes glittered like jade behind the dark lenses as she twisted from side to side in her efforts to identify the buildings from her guide book, but after a while she gave up and just gazed as one beautiful building succeeded another along the Grand Canal, some of them in sore need of facelifts, others in all the glory of recent restoration, with mooring posts like gaily striped barbers' poles at their canal-side entrances.

'But some of the buildings have flowers and plants trailing from them,' she exclaimed in surprise. 'Somehow I never expected greenery as well as all this incredible architecture.' She halted suddenly at the look of amusement on his face. 'I sound like a schoolgirl,' she said resignedly.

'No. Just refreshingly enthusiastic,' he contradicted. 'You let me see Venice through new eyes—not that I really need to. Its particular allure never fails for me, prosaic engineer though I am.'

Olivia smiled at him wryly. 'When we met yesterday the last thing I expected was a day in your company today. Your opening gambit was pretty offensive.'

'I was tired and angry and you were my only possible clue as to what had happened to Drew. If I was rude I apologise.'

'Accepted,' she said, then gasped as they rounded a corner to see a building with a superb stone staircase spiralling upwards from a tiny square at the water's edge. 'What's that?'

'The Palazzo Contarini dal Bovolo,' Max informed her. 'Pure Renaissance, built at the end of the fifteenth century—incredible structure.'

By this time the *vaporetto* was very crowded, though Max made sure Olivia kept her vantage point each time another wave of passengers crammed into the vessel. He kept one arm locked behind her, with a hand on the rail, and at first Olivia was very conscious of the casual proximity to a man she'd only met a few hours before, then she forgot all about it as the tall campanile of San Marco and the Doge's Palace came into view. She alighted from the *vaporetto* in silence among the noisy crowds, gazing in unashamed wonder at the buildings, oblivious to the heat until Max led her towards a hat stall where a jovial, admiring man handed her various styles to try on, providing a mirror for her to view the result.

'Take the big one,' advised Max. 'The ribbon matches your eyes.'

'Thank you,' said Olivia politely, surprised he'd noticed they were green. 'Right then, Mr Guide, take me to the Basilica San Marco for starters, then I'd like a coffee in one of those cafes along the *piazza*, and afterwards, just to make you sorry you ever volunteered for the job, I'd like a look at some shops. All part of the service I provide in my reports,' she added, grinning at him.

'After a couple of months surrounded by oil, sand and camels I'm perfectly happy to look at shops,' he said, surprising her. 'In fact, perhaps you'll help me buy a present for Sarah.'

They spent a long time in the awesome interior of San Marco, where Olivia ran out of superlatives as she gazed at the Pala d'Oro, the golden screen behind the main altar where the sarcophagus of St Mark rested.

'Look at the enamel work,' said Max softly. 'The craftsmanship and the subjects are supposed to reflect the Venetian spirit and faith as well as their superb taste.'

Olivia nodded dumbly, though she grew more talkative when she saw the mosaic of Salome above the Baptistry, captivated by the extraordinary allure in the slender figure in the clinging dress.

'No wonder Herod gave her what she asked for,' she whispered.

'Something one should be careful about,' commented Max, eyeing the mosaic.

'What one asks for?'

'Exactly—in case one gets it.'

Olivia gave a little shiver. 'I think I could do with some very secular coffee after all this, Max, please. I find I can only take in so much culture at a time.'

Later, after admiring the clock tower while the two bronze Moors on top of it struck the great bell at eleven, they sat for a pleasant interlude, drinking coffee as they watched the world go by among the pigeons on the vast *piazza*. Afterwards Max led Olivia along narrow streets lined with shops, interspersed here and there with the inevitable bridges over the canals. She hung over one in delight when she spotted a gondola complete with wheelbarrow and cement as workmen made repairs to one of the buildings.

'What it must cost to bring everything in by boat!'

'Too true. I'm glad I'm not responsible for this little lot.'

Contrary to her preconceived idea of him, Max Hamilton was commendably patient as Olivia gazed at elegant, expensive clothes in the windows of shops with famous couturier names, but after a while she smiled in apology.

'You must be bored rigid. And you mentioned something about a present for Sarah. What did you have in mind?'

He shrugged. 'Something unbreakable and not too bulky to take home in the plane, I suppose.'

Shortly afterwards they found a shop selling table-cloths, blouses and baby clothes, all the articles exquisitely hand-embroidered.

'This could be your answer,' said Olivia, peering at the price on the largest of the cloths. She whipped out her calculator and worked out the price in sterling, then whistled. 'I'm amazed. For a twelve-place setting with napkins, and all that exquisite white embroidery and lace insertion, it's a bargain, I promise you. Sarah's cup of tea, do you think?'

Max shrugged. 'She's a good cook, does quite a bit of entertaining. I think you've hit on exactly the right thing. Let's go in and haggle.'

'Haggle!' protested Olivia as they went in. 'It's a very good price already,' she hissed as an elegant young man came forward to greet them.

Max smiled at her lazily, and in fluent Italian began on a bargaining session enjoyed on both sides, the result satisfactory all round.

'I just can't bargain like that,' sighed Olivia later, as they lingered at a shop window displaying oils and water-colours by local artists.

'If you fancy something in here I'm more than willing to go into my routine again,' he offered.

Olivia peered at one of the price-tickets and winced. 'No amount of haggling would bring *that* into my price range.'

'Then let me treat you to lunch at Harry's Bar,' suggested Max as they continued walking.

Olivia frowned. 'But surely it's hideously expensive there—isn't that where Hemingway used to hang out?'

'Right on both counts, but after a spell in the desert—relatively speaking—I consider myself entitled to a fleshpot or two.' He stopped in front of a very inconspicuous doorway. 'Here we are.'

Olivia, who would have walked straight past, followed Max inside and up the stairs to the main dining-room, where the head waiter greeted her escort with a warm smile.

'Signor Hamilton, welcome. How nice to see you again.'

Max returned the greeting then introduced Olivia, explaining that it was the lady's first time in Venice.

In seconds they were seated at a corner table with a view across the Grand Canal, while white-jacketed waiters circled round them, flicking out starched peach linen napkins, filling glasses with mineral water, setting down dishes of black olives and butter and circular brioche-type rolls as light as air for Olivia to nibble at while Max looked at the wine list.

'Are you likely to choose meat or fish?' he enquired.

'I had fish last night—I quite fancy some chicken,' she said, studying the menu.

'Right.' Max had a quick-fire exchange in Italian with the wine waiter, then ran his eye down the list of dishes on offer.

'Eating's obviously a serious business in this part of the world,' said Olivia. Constantly amazed that everything looked so utterly familiar, she gazed happily at the fabulously beautiful view of the Salute church across the canal.

Max chuckled. 'To me Venice is always synonymous with indulgence of appetite, both food and beauty—like a great big iced cake that gives you indigestion if you try to take in too much of it at a time. But talking of food, have you decided?'

Olivia nodded, firmly refusing a first course. Tempted by the *sampietro*, the fillet of John Dory with peppers, she finally settled on chicken and ordered *pollo cacciatora* with *polenta*, Max opting for *tagliolini ai funghi* to start followed by *fegato di vitello*.

'Pasta with mushrooms, then calf's liver,' he explained.

Olivia pulled a face, then looked at the fellow diners as Max gave their order. 'Do you think any of these people are local celebrities?' she whispered.

'They probably think they are,' he returned sardonically. 'But I don't recognise anyone. You'll have to be content with memories of Hemingway and Orson Welles, plus Winston Churchill, of course. He used to call in here after his painting expeditions.'

She smiled at him. 'Thank you for bringing me here today. If I'd come alone I'd never have found this place—or come inside on my own, even, if I had.'

'Why not?'

She looked around her at the surprisingly simple surroundings, the peach-painted walls half panelled in dark wood, the black and white photographs of famous American landmarks. 'I travel a lot, and eat alone a lot, but some places I'd never go into alone. This is one of them. But at least I'll be able to describe it now to anyone wanting to know the smart places to frequent in Venice.' She turned her eyes on the darkly tanned face of the man watching her. 'At least Venice has taken my mind off worries about Sophie for a while.'

Max nodded, and drank some of his wine. 'I was just thinking the same thing about Drew. In the cold light of day I realise that if he refuses to come home with me there's damn all I can do about it. He's a grown man.'

'At least you can tell him to behave like a civilised human being and let Sarah know what's happening.'

'And how will you feel if he intends transferring his affections to your sister?' asked Max grimly. His dark eyes held Olivia's for a moment.

She looked away, shrugging. 'Guilty, I imagine. Which is ridiculous. I'm not my sister's keeper.'

'No, you're not. I vote we forget our respective siblings for today, and concentrate on Venice. She deserves undivided attention.'

Olivia nodded in agreement, summoning a smile as a waiter arrived with a large dish of pasta. Despite her protests he insisted on serving her with a small portion before serving Max.

'Oh, but I really didn't want——' she began, but the waiter, who had light blue eyes and a very attractive smile informed her that the *funghi* were the first of the *porcini*, the mushrooms much prized locally, and the *signora* must taste just a little.

'He's right,' said Olivia ruefully, after the first mouthful. 'This is wonderful! If I stay too long in this part of the world I'll need a crash diet when I get home.'

Max flicked a glance at the curves outlined in fawn silk, and applied himself to his plate. 'I think there's a long way to go before you need worry on that score.'

'I wasn't fishing,' she said tartly.

'I know.' He raised a sardonic eyebrow. 'Why should you need to? Compliments can hardly be a rarity to someone with looks like yours.'

'More than you think,' she said shortly, and laid down her fork. 'A pity, but if I eat any more I shan't have room for my *cacciatora*.'

'Try some of the wine,' he advised. 'Oddly enough Venice isn't particularly renowned for wine, but this white is quite pleasant.'

Olivia accepted half a glass, then returned to her study of the other patrons of the restaurant, noting that without exception the women were all skilfully made up and dressed with that mixture of elegance and restraint which seemed to typify Venetian style.

'What would you like to do after lunch?' asked Max as the waiter took their plates. 'I've made my purchase, but so far you haven't bought a thing.'

'I'd like something in leather for my father, I think. He scolds if I take back presents every trip, but he must have something from Venice.'

'What does your father do?'

'He used to be a language master at the local boys' school, but he's retired now. These days he works in the garden, reads a lot, umpires cricket matches, plays chess with a crony and has a walk down to the local for a lunchtime pint sometimes when it's fine.' Olivia smiled affectionately. 'He's one of the many in retirement who can't think how they had time to go to work.'

Their main course arrived, and for a while there was silence as Olivia savoured the subtle flavours of her chicken dish.

'Though I don't think I'll ever go a bundle on the spongy stuff served with it. What is it?' she asked.

'*Polenta*—excellent filling material for hungry stomachs.'

'You can say that again!' Once again Oliva laid down her fork before her plate was empty.

'Didn't you enjoy it?' asked Max, polishing off thin strips of liver with gusto.

'Very much, but I'm determined to sample one of those delectable puddings on that trolley over there.' Olivia grinned at him. 'I don't eat pudding as a rule, but I think I owe it to my clients to report on the offerings at Harry's Bar.'

'Have you been told your eyes shine like jewels when the sun's on them?' said Max conversationally, killing Olivia's smile stone-dead.

'Not often,' she said coolly.

'You don't care for compliments?'

'Not about my looks, anyway—they're just an accident of birth.' She turned away deliberately, glad when the blue-eyed waiter caused a diversion by replacing the tablecloth with a fresh one for the dessert course as the head waiter wheeled the trolley to the table.

'Which would madam care for?' said the latter, but Olivia had already made her choice earlier from a distance, succumbing to the allure of a sinfully dark, rich chocolate cake.

'Aren't you having anything?' she asked Max, fork poised.

'No. I ate far more of the *porcini* pasta, remember. I'll join you in a coffee when you've eaten that.'

The cake was hardly a cake at all, merely wafer-thin slices of featherlight sponge layered with cream and the darkest, richest icing Olivia had ever tasted.

'I feel very guilty, but it was worth it,' she said at last, as she laid down her fork with a sigh.

'Why guilty?' he asked, amused.

Olivia hesitated, her eyes meeting his. 'I couldn't help noticing the prices. Would you be offended if I offered to pay my share?'

'I certainly would,' said Max brusquely.

Her lips twitched. 'Then I won't!'

They lingered a little over coffee, then went out at last into the blazing Venetian afternoon, glad to keep to shaded back streets as they wandered round shops just beginning to open again after their protracted lunch-hour.

Olivia found a wallet for her father in one of them, treated herself to an irresistible glass goblet in a deep ruby red in another, by which time she was rather weary.

'I know I should go and look at more churches, or at the very least an art gallery,' she said, yawning, 'but would you think it very rude if I suggested we catch a *vaporetto* back fairly soon? I see what you mean about Venice as an indulgence. I feel I've taken in enough of it for one day.'

CHAPTER THREE

OLIVIA was glad to relinquish the car keys to Max on the way back, unsurprised to find he was a fast, skilful driver who knew the area well, with no need to look for road signs on the way back to the Villa Bellagio.

'Thank you,' she said, as he slowed on the approach to the impressive entrance to the grounds, giving her time to admire the pair of Roman statues on the stone pillars. Max brought the car to a halt under the trees shading one side of the drive in front of the hotel, then strolled slowly with her towards the white façade of the Villa, where a row of stone urns filled with scarlet geraniums flanked the open glass doors of the entrance.

'You look tired,' he commented.

'Ridiculous, really,' she said ruefully. 'Holidays are so tiring. I get less weary in work.'

'Your problem is nervous strain, plus your first introduction to Venice,' he pointed out wryly. 'Have a long nap before dinner.'

'First I'm going for a swim!' Olivia collected her key, smiling at Floria, the receptionist. 'Any messages?'

'No, *signora*,' said the girl apologetically. 'But there is one for you, Signor Hamilton.'

Max read the note, his face darkening. 'Just another call from Sarah,' he said in response to Olivia's querying look. 'Nothing from Drew, damn him.'

'But he doesn't know you're here, remember.'

39

'I've left messages with the television people, on his answering machine and everywhere I can think of,' he said grimly. 'If he's been in contact with anyone he'll know I'm on his track.'

'You'll probably catch up with him tomorrow.' Olivia felt a reluctant pang of sympathy for the missing Drew at the look on Max's face.

'I bloody well hope so,' he growled, as they left the hall for the colonnade. 'But no more talk about the runaways. Would you have dinner with me this evening?'

Olivia glanced at him warily as they climbed the smooth stone stairs to the upper floor. 'You needn't feel obligated as far as I'm concerned, just because of Sophie—and Drew,' she said quietly.

'In other words, you don't want to,' he said brusquely.

'Are you always so touchy?'

He scowled. 'What do you mean—touchy? I asked a perfectly simple question and you gave me the kind of oblique answer women use when they're too polite to say no.'

'Oh for heaven's sake,' she said impatiently. 'I was afraid *you* were just being polite, that's all.'

'I'm hardly ever polite,' he said, thawing.

'I had noticed!'

'I'll meet you at eight in the bar.'

Once in her room Olivia was tempted to stretch out on the bed and take a nap, but the allure of the pool below was too strong. Minutes later, with a white towelling robe over her jade-green swimsuit, she ran downstairs, towel over her arm, and made for an empty deckchair. The pool had very few occupants this late, though several people were sunbathing on the chairs, or reading, or just dozing in the sun, which had lost its earlier ferocity and gave out a pleasant warmth perfect for a pre-dinner swim. Olivia tied up her hair, slid out of her robe and made for the side of the pool, where she dived neatly into the deep end.

Propelling herself through the water with a leisurely backstroke, Olivia gazed up at the deepening blue of the sky, trying to empty her mind of the ever-present worry about Sophie and what awaited her in Pordenone the following day. One day at a time, she told herself, and swam to the side of the pool, where a muscular brown arm took her by surprise as it reached down to help her out.

Max, dripping water like herself, grinned down at her. 'When you mentioned a swim it seemed like a good idea. It was my main form of relaxation in Qatar. The temperature of the water there is so high it's like taking a warm bath. This your towel?'

Olivia nodded, glad to take refuge in the white, fleecy folds, finding herself as embarrassed as a schoolgirl at the proximity to the half-naked male body burned dark by a fiercer sun than anything that shone on Venice.

She shrugged into her robe quickly as Max dried himself. 'I didn't notice you swimming in there.'

'You were probably thinking about your sister,' he said soberly. 'I watched you for a while before I went in.'

'Actually I was telling myself not to think about her at all until tomorrow,' said Olivia briskly.

'Good idea.' Max wrapped himself in a robe similar to hers. 'Are you going in now, or are you going to lie in the sun for a while?'

'If I want my hair to look civilised by dinnertime I'd better make a start on it right now,' she said regretfully. 'Pity. It's absolutely perfect out here at this hour.'

He nodded. 'I'll sit awhile, then have another swim before I go up. See you later.'

Olivia smiled and strolled away across the lawn, half wishing she'd stayed, then frowned, surprised by how much she'd wanted to. Strange! Max Hamilton was totally unlike the type of man she usually gravitated towards. But then, how many men *had* she felt attracted to lately? Absolutely none. For which there was good reason. One she wanted to think about even less than the approaching showdown with Sophie tomorrow.

Olivia made it a habit to travel light on her research expeditions, and if she'd been dining alone would have kept to the clothes of the night before. Dinner with Max seemed to call for more effort, though in the mood he'd been in when they first met, she thought with a wry smile, Max wouldn't have noticed if she'd been wearing a potato sack last night. Rather to her own surprise, she even plugged in her travel iron to remove the creases from the olive-green shantung dress she decided on before standing under the shower to shampoo her hair. Afterwards she treated her hair and face to such lavish attention that she gave herself a warning look in the mirror, aware that it was a long time since she'd felt such anticipation over spending an evening with any man. And Max Hamilton, of all men, was not the most appropriate choice, since he could hardly fail to cause a great big upset in her family before another twenty-four hours elapsed. Sufficient unto the day, she told herself flatly.

Whatever happened tomorrow, there was no reason why this evening shouldn't be a very pleasant way of passing the time. Pordenone, the Villa Nerone and whatever crisis awaited her there would keep until tomorrow.

Having taken such unusual time and trouble over her appearance, she found Max's reaction very gratifying when she joined him later in the bar.

He swept dark, approving eyes over her as he led her to a sofa. 'You look wonderful, Olivia. Tell me,' he added, a smile playing at the corners of his mouth. 'Do you always match your clothes to those fabulous eyes of yours?'

'More often than not,' she said casually.

He laughed and asked the waiter for a bottle of champagne.

'Champagne?' she said quickly. 'Have you heard from Drew? Are you celebrating?'

'No word from Drew, but I thought the champagne was a good idea anyway, just to mark the occasion,' he told her, as the waiter drew the cork from some vintage Veuve Clicquot with panache.

'What occasion?' asked Olivia, when they were alone.

Max, who was wearing a lightweight fawn suit with a crisp white shirt and rust red silk tie, had obviously taken trouble with his own appearance. He looked at her with unnerving directness, no trace of smile softening the hardness of his features. 'You're a beautiful, intelligent woman, Olivia, and I've enjoyed your company today. But tomorrow I'm probably going to make your little sister very unhappy, and when that happens I don't hold out much hope of any further social contact where you and I are concerned. So tonight is special, a one-off deserving of vintage champagne as an overture to the finest offerings of the Bellagio chef, and an evening spent with a lady I wish I'd met in very different circumstances.' He raised his glass in toast. 'To your beautiful green eyes, Olivia Maitland.'

Olivia sat silent while he drank, then raised her own glass, her pulse rather more rapid than usual. 'Your very good health, Max Hamilton.'

'Right,' he said briskly, 'now we've got that out of the way, tell me how you enjoyed your first sight of Venice.'

In response to Max's directness, Olivia told him frankly that his company had added enormously to her enjoyment of the excursion. 'I wouldn't have ventured so far, or lunched so royally on my own,' she said, smiling. 'Thank you for a lovely day.'

'Which is a long way from over,' he pointed out, and refilled her glass.

Olivia sipped from it sparingly, telling him she'd pored over her guide-book while she dried her hair, finding out the names of the buildings which had impressed her most. 'Though apart from St Mark's Basilica and the Doge's Palace, I think I'll remember the one with the spiral stair most vividly.'

'You need to come back to Venice again and again,' said Max. 'Today was the merest skim over the surface.'

'I'd like a trip in a gondola, and a look round more galleries and churches next time,' she told him. 'Though heaven knows when that will be.'

'You mentioned three hotels on this trip. Where do you go after Pordenone?'

'Asolo, in the foothills, the town where Robert Browning wrote "Pippa Passes". I'm staying at the Villa Cipriani, which was once his home for a while, and which these days can boast the Queen Mother as a guest.' Olivia smiled. 'My boss usually samples such exalted watering places himself, but this time he's entrusted a report on it to me.'

'And after that?'

'I go back to my flat in Ealing, which is near enough to the travel agency for me to walk to work every day. My father lives near Cheltenham, and Sophie divides her time between us, when she's not in college. This past year she's been over here, of course, and we've missed her badly.' Olivia changed the subject abruptly, waving away the champagne bottle Max proffered. 'No more, or I won't be able to handle a knife and fork!'

'Then let's eat,' he said promptly.

To dine with Max for company made the evening a far more special occasion than the previous one, Olivia acknowledged secretly. Twenty-four hours before she hadn't even met him, she thought, smiling at him over the melon and *prosciutto crudo* she chose for her first course. And their first meeting had hardly been idyllic. If someone had told her she'd be dining tonight with the angry, hostile man who'd been so brusque with her the night before she wouldn't have believed it. Yet here they were at a candle-lit table looking out on the floodlit gardens, with a waxing moon reflected in the pool, and she was enjoying Max Hamilton's company to a degree she knew was rather rash in the circumstances. She thrust the thought to the back of her mind as she ate the lobster which followed, then looked up at him, startled, as Max asked bluntly if there was a man in her life.

'No,' she said after a slight pause.

'Why the hesitation?'

'I was about to add "not now".'

'I didn't imagine a woman like you would have reached your age without several men in her life,' he said, leaning back in his chair.

'What age do you think that is?' she parried lightly.

'You told me Sophie's twenty and you were nineteen when she was ten.' His teeth gleamed in his dark face. 'Why so surprised?'

'I didn't expect you to remember the details.' She smiled back. 'I'd have told you anyway. I shall be thirty in September, if you want the exact statistics, but my age is the least of my concerns.'

'As well it might be. I can give you nine years or so, but I don't consider myself totally decrepit as yet.'

Olivia eyed the tall, lounging figure in amusement.

'What's so funny?' he demanded.

'I was just thinking anything less decrepit would be hard to imagine.'

'Thank you, ma'am,' he drawled, and leaned forward. 'Tell me, Olivia, why was there such an odd look on your face when I asked you if you always wore green?'

She waited for a moment before answering, taking advantage of the pause as the waiter removed their plates.

'Someone close to me had only one superstition in his life. He jeered at Friday the thirteenth and walked under ladders, but he was adamant that the colour green was a jinx in his life. He survived a very bad crash in the only green car he'd ever possessed, and from then on it was a colour he couldn't bear.'

'How did he feel about your eyes?' asked Max curiously, his brows drawn together.

'Since they were a fixture he put up with them,' said Olivia wryly, 'but he made such a fuss if I bought anything green to wear that I got out of the habit. Life was easier that way. These days I wear it as a sort of symbol of my independence, I suppose.'

'Did you love this guy?'

'Yes. Once.'

'But no more?'

'No.'

'Do you still see him?'

'No.'

'In other words it's none of my business!'

'Not exactly. It's just a subject I don't like discussing. How about you?' she added firmly. 'Do you have someone in *your* life?'

'Not at the moment. I lived with someone for several years, actually, but somehow the relationship went off the boil. With mutual regret we decided to call it a day.' He gave her a crooked smile. 'I enjoy other more ephemeral relationships, of course, I'm not a monk, but my peripatetic lifestyle doesn't really lend itself to permanence. Which is why I'm settling down at the UK headquarters and sending other people all over the globe for a change. Lately I've got a yen to put down roots, live in the same place and never open a suitcase between one holiday and the next.'

'Won't you be bored?'

'I don't know yet. But it's time I found out.' He smiled as a waiter approached to offer them dessert. 'Are you in the mood for more sinful indulgence?'

Olivia shook her head, smiling. 'Once in a while is more than enough for that kind of thing. But I'd like some coffee. Could we have it here and watch the moon set over those trees there?'

'Whatever you want,' he assured her, looking round to find most of the tables deserted.

'Do you suppose they'd prefer us to drink it in the bar?'

'No idea,' he said indifferently. 'If you want your coffee here we'll stay as long as you like.'

Olivia felt relaxed, finding it very pleasant to engage in idle conversation backed by a chorus of chirruping crickets from the scented, floodlit garden as they drained the coffee pot dry. But at last she took pity on the waiters obviously waiting to clear away, and suggested they take a walk.

'It's such a beautiful night it's a shame to go in just yet,' she said as they strolled along the lamp-lit avenues of the formal gardens, where statues glimmered palely amongst the greenery.

'When you go back to this flat of yours, do you live in it alone?' asked Max.

'Yes.'

'You're never lonely?'

She gave him an amused look as they passed through a circle of light from one of the lamps. 'Of course I get lonely. But never enough to want to share again. Besides, Dad comes to stay with me now and then, and so does Sophie. And I have friends I see on a regular basis.'

'It all sounds very minor-key for someone like you,' he commented.

'What do you mean, someone like me?'

Max paused in the darkness between two pools of light. 'You're a very beautiful woman, Olivia, with intelligence to match. There must be men queuing up to take you anywhere you want.'

Olivia looked up at him thoughtfully. 'I have men *friends*, who wine and dine me fairly regularly, just as I return the compliment by giving them a meal at my place occasionally. But never with something extra to round off the evening.'

He threw up a hand like a fencer. 'Actually, I didn't mean that. It just seems extraordinary to me that a woman of your attraction leads a life more suited to someone about forty years older.'

Olivia threw back her head and laughed. 'Oh, dear, I did make it sound dull. Actually my life suits me perfectly, I promise you.'

'No thoughts of marriage?'

'No.' She shrugged. 'Since we're not likely to meet again after tomorrow I suppose there's no harm in telling you I left the important bit out about the man who hated green. I was married to him.'

His eyes narrowed. 'Was? You're divorced?'

'No. I'm a widow.'

'Hell—I'm sorry,' he said gruffly, and took her hand. 'I didn't mean to rake up tragic memories.'

'You didn't,' she said candidly. 'The marriage was a disaster from the word go. We married in haste and almost immediately began the proverbial repenting at leisure—to the extent that when Anthony died all I could feel was a sense of release.'

'Was this recent?' asked Max, halting.

'Four years ago.' Olivia looked up at him. 'Strange—I never believed that it's easier to confide in strangers. But it's true. Normally I can't bring myself to talk about it.' She smiled crookedly. 'Maybe you missed your vocation. You might have made a good priest.'

'I seriously doubt it!' His fingers tightened on hers. 'People don't usually find me easy to confide in, believe me. And other aspects of the calling have no appeal at all.'

'Poverty? Obedience?' she parried.

'Both of those,' he agreed, 'but celibacy is my main objection—don't pull away. You've nothing to fear from me.'

'No,' she agreed, as they resumed their strolling. 'If I thought so I wouldn't be out here with you right now.'

'Which doesn't mean you're not the most attractive woman I've met in a long, long time,' he went on conversationally. 'I could wring Drew's neck!'

'Why?'

'If we'd just met like any two people encountering each other in the normal way I could ask you for your telephone number and get in touch when we get back to the UK. Whereas after tomorrow the last thing you'll want is anything to do with any of the Hamilton family.'

'I don't hold you responsible,' she assured him.

'For which many thanks. But once the balloon goes up when I catch up with Drew and your sister relations are unlikely to be cordial between you and me, Olivia Maitland.'

'True,' she admitted honestly, then hesitated. 'Look, do you want a lift to the Villa Nerone in the morning?'

Max stopped, staring down at her in the brighter light near the hotel entrance. 'You mean that?'

'I rarely say things I don't mean.'

'You know damn well I want to travel with you.' He gave her a twisted smile. 'At the risk of getting my head bitten off, I was going to suggest it anyway.'

'Then I've saved you the trouble,' she said lightly, wishing she'd waited for him to ask.

'I'll pay my share of the hire fee.'

'No—my firm sees to all that—besides, you paid for lunch *and* dinner,' she pointed out.

They went through the hall together and out into the shadowy colonnade, both of them rather silent as they mounted the steps and walked towards her room.

'Thank you for dinner. Goodnight,' said Olivia rather breathlessly. She put her key in the lock then held out her hand to him.

Max took the hand, held it in his for a long moment while he stared down at her in the gloom. He took her by surprise when he raised it to his lips, then surprised her a great deal more by pulling her into his arms and kissing her square on her open, surprised mouth. 'After tomorrow I'll probably never see you again,' he muttered against her lips, and kissed them again.

The startling discovery that she hated the very thought of parting with him next day vanquished any opposition from Olivia, and Max's arms tightened, his seeking, expert mouth inciting a hot rush of response she felt right down to her toes. For an unmeasured, fast-breathing, pulse-racing interval they

shared an embrace which blotted out their surroundings, until the sound of voices and approaching
footsteps on the stone stairs acted like two giant hands
which tore them apart, and Olivia, hot-cheeked and
embarrassed as a schoolgirl, muttered something incoherent and escaped into her room.

CHAPTER FOUR

IN HER room Olivia packed with savage swiftness, in such unaccustomed turmoil that she needed occupation to calm herself down. What, she demanded of herself bitterly, had she been thinking about? The heated exchange just now had been so far removed from a mere goodnight kiss that she had no idea how she was going to face Max in the morning, especially as she'd been the one to ask him to share the journey, not the other way round. It wasn't even full moon! She had no excuse at all for behaving like—Olivia paused, eyes narrowed. Like Sophie? she asked herself. Her sister, at least, was only twenty years old and had the excuse of immaturity to offer for her actions. With almost ten years' seniority and a failed marriage under your belt, Olivia Maitland, she told her reflection in the bathroom mirror, you should have behaved with more sense.

The telephone interrupted her self-disgust. Olivia dived across the room to pick up the receiver.

'Sophie?' she demanded, breathlessly.

'No, it's Max.'

Olivia sat down on the bed with a thump.

'Are you still there?' he asked sharply.

'Yes—yes, of course.'

'I haven't rung to apologise,' he informed her.

'Oh.'

'Nor,' he went on sardonically, 'to demand entry to your room, if that's why you're breathless.'

'I was in the bathroom. I ran.'

There was silence for a moment, then, 'Olivia,' said Max gruffly, 'you were obviously upset when you dived for cover.'

'Upset!' she retorted with sarcasm. 'I was angry.'

'With me?'

'No, with me.'

'I didn't mean to kiss you—lord knows I've wanted to all day. I defy any man to look at your face—that mouth—and *not* want to kiss you, but it wasn't planned. It just happened.'

'Are you telling me this because you're afraid I'll renege on the arrangement to drive you to Pordenone?'

'Oddly enough,' he said stiffly, 'that didn't cross my mind. You were obviously embarrassed just now. I wanted to put that right. I'm obviously not succeeding.'

'Yes, you are,' she said, relenting. 'You're right. I was quite extraordinarily embarrassed.'

'Why?'

'*Why?*' She breathed in audibly. 'I don't usually— I mean, you took me by surprise and—and I——'

'Gave way to a completely natural impulse that proved so enjoyable neither of us remembered we were in a public place,' he said matter-of-factly.

Olivia bit her lip, suddenly feeling a little ridiculous. 'Exactly,' she said ruefully. 'Thank you for ringing.'

'I would have come in person,' he informed her drily, 'but I thought you might misconstrue my motives.'

She laughed. 'True. I'm not a very trusting person.'

'You can trust me,' he said without emphasis.

'Good,' she said briskly. 'See you in the morning, then.'

'Eight sharp,' he ordered, then added, 'please!' and Olivia laughed.

'Oh, much better! Goodnight.'

When she put the phone down, she yawned widely, suddenly feeling so very much better after Max's call that she abandoned any further preparations for the night and crawled into bed, asleep almost the moment her head touched the pillow.

When Olivia joined Max next morning, dressed ready for travelling in olive cotton trousers and white, olive-striped shirt, any constraint she might have felt was dispelled by the spirited discussion on football Max was conducting with the two waiters serving breakfast.

'*Buon giorno*,' she said to the waiters, and smiled at Max.

'Good morning,' he said, holding out her chair for her. 'Did you sleep well?'

'Much better than I expected,' she said frankly, pouring coffee for them both. 'Thank you for ringing,' she added.

Max buttered a roll, eyeing her. 'I meant to the moment I got in the room, but Sarah got in first with another demand for news. She got quite stroppy with me because I confessed to a day in Venice instead of combing the neighbourhood for Drew. I had to get her in a calmer state of mind before I could talk to you.'

'You must have been glad to get to sleep,' said Olivia, pulling a face.

'I didn't for some time,' he said morosely.

'Worried about Drew?'

Max turned dark, very direct eyes on her. 'That too.'

Her cheeks warm, Olivia poured herself more coffee hastily and brought out her map, asking his advice on the best route to Pordenone.

'Don't worry about that,' he said casually. 'I know the area. I'll drive.'

'You obviously disapproved of my driving skills yesterday,' she said tartly, putting the map away.

'Not at all. It's not far, but you'll be less tired when you get there if I take the wheel. You'll probably need to be,' he added grimly.

Olivia sighed, and refilled the cup he held out. 'I confess I'm not looking forward to the encounter. Sophie's bound to hate me for putting her wise about your brother.'

'Maybe Sarah's the one who'll be doing the hating,' he pointed out. 'Drew may very well be so enamoured of your sister he'll dig his heels in, wedding or no wedding.'

'That won't happen,' said Olivia with conviction. 'Once Sophie hears about Sarah she'll send him packing.'

'Will she?' said Max as their eyes met.

Olivia felt suddenly cold. 'Of course she will!' She jumped to her feet, suddenly unable to sit there any longer. 'I'm off to settle my bill,' she said. 'See you at the car in fifteen minutes.'

The Villa Nerone was very different from the Bellagio. Situated much farther outside the town of Pordenone than Olivia expected, the original building was as old as the other hotel, but it had been modernised and added to, with a whole new wing carefully constructed to blend with the original villa. Once again there was an imposing entrance with pillars topped by statues, but part of the grounds had been turned into a car park, discreetly hidden behind an avenue of trees. It was mid-morning by the time they arrived. Max parked the car in the shade and took Olivia's overnight bag from the car with his own luggage just as the clock in the campanile of the local church struck eleven.

'How long do you mean to stay here?' he asked as they walked towards the main entrance building.

'I'm booked for two nights then I go on to Asolo,' said Olivia. 'Originally Sophie was supposed to stay with me, but now your guess is as good as mine as to what happens next. How about you?'

'I wish I knew,' said Max grimly. 'I'll book in for one night, anyway.'

'Can't you stay in your stepmother's house? Isn't that nearby somewhere?'

'It's a fair distance, actually. I'll need to hire a car unless I can hitch a lift with Drew in the Cobra.' His mouth tightened. 'Not that I fancy that idea much, for obvious reasons.'

At the desk in the foyer Olivia confirmed her booking and signed the register, then asked the receptionist if there were any messages for her.

'*Si, signora*,' said the girl. 'I have one from Miss Sophie Collins. She says she will be here at twelve-thirty. I will ring you when she arrives.'

Olivia followed the porter with Max, too uptight to take much note of the recently refurbished surroundings, other than an impression of lavish gilt and marble as she mounted the stairs in the annexe. The corridors leading to the bedrooms were thickly carpeted, and the chill of air conditioning made her shiver as they were shown to adjoining rooms.

Max sent the porter on his way with a generous tip, then eyed Olivia questioningly. 'There's a bar downstairs. When you've settled in, give me a knock. I suggest we go down and wait for them there over a drink. You'll go mad doing nothing in here for an hour.'

Olivia gave a cursory glance round the luxuriously furnished room. 'Cable television, no less. Rather different from the Bellagio.'

'Not your type of thing?'

'Everyone to their own taste—and some of my customers might prefer the more modern touches.' Olivia smiled rather wanly, tense now confrontation with Sophie was at hand. 'Thank you for driving me here. I feel a bit untidy after the journey—I need a shower before I come down."

Max took her hand in his, a look of command in his eyes. 'I'll give you ten minutes, then I come hammering on the door. Understood?'

She smiled unwillingly, and he nodded, satisfied.

'That's more like it.'

It was more like twenty minutes before Olivia had showered, found some fresh underwear and a crisp white cotton shirt. She made up her face swiftly, brushed her hair and slid her feet into flat bronze pumps in place of the canvas ones worn on the journey. She sprayed herself with perfume, then opened the door just as Max Hamilton, also in fresh white shirt and khakis, raised his hand to knock on it.

'Ready?'

She nodded, and locked her door, walking with him in silence along the thickly carpeted corridors enclosed by rooms on either side.

'A lot different from the Bellagio,' she commented.

'I fancy your dread of what's coming would colour your opinion of this place however beautiful it was,' he said wryly, as they went down the stairs to the marble and gilt foyer.

'You're probably right.' Olivia took out her notebook when they were settled at a table on the cloistered terrace outside. 'But it's very comfortable and well-appointed so I suppose I may as well note down the pluses here before I get overtaken by events.'

Max ordered coffee from the hovering waiter, then waved a hand at the manicured lawn and the ancient, picturesque church just in view beyond the pillared hotel entrance. 'This should appeal to the punters, surely! Mention that the nearby village is medieval, with a ninth century gate in its walls. Throw in the Goldoni plays they put on there in the open-air theatre alongside the church, and you can't fail.'

'You've obviously been here before.'

'Not to stay. I brought Luisa for a meal here one night when I was passing through.'

'I thought you weren't on those kinds of terms.'

'If my work brings me to Italy, as it does on occasion, I feel obliged to look Luisa up, if only for my father's sake. She made him very happy, and I'm grateful to her for that even if she and I don't always see eye to eye—especially when it comes to her darling boy.'

'And is Drew just as attentive to his mother?'

'Far more so. He's a typical Italian son in that respect, thinks the world of Luisa, still calls her "Mamma", even at his age.'

Olivia smiled, surprised. 'Remembering the personality he projects on television, that's hard to picture, somehow.'

Max lounged back in his chair, long legs stretched out in front of him. 'Drew is like a chameleon, all things to all people. To Sophie he's probably a knight errant who carried her off in the Cobra in lieu of a white horse.'

Olivia, more disturbed than ever by this thumbnail sketch of Drew Hamilton, applied herself determinedly to her notebook, recording her impressions so far of the Villa Nerone.

'Would you say this was the sort of place a party of women could come to for a holiday?' she asked, looking up.

'Does that happen much these days?' asked Max in surprise.

'You have been out of it lately! Hen holidays are very much the fashion in certain circles. A lot of women come to me for reassurance on suitable places to stay without their male partners.'

'Which must rule out quite a few corners of the globe, I imagine,' he said drily.

'Italy's fine.' Olivia smiled suddenly, her eyes dancing. 'The men are known to be attentive, but respectful.'

Max's eyes held hers, one of his eyebrows raised sardonically. 'But not impervious to a smile like that, so watch yourself. Try not to impose too great a strain on male restraint, Italian or any other variety, when you're travelling alone.'

'I do it often enough to know the form,' she retorted. 'I do have a brain, you know, *and* use it whenever possible.' She got up, putting her notebook away. 'I'm going up to my room for a while. It's very hot here. Are you going to wait for the truant stepbrother right here?'

'Yes,' said Max, on his feet. 'Stay with me, Olivia. This may be the last time we spend any time alone together.'

She gave him a wry little smile. 'You won't believe this, but I have the beginnings of a crashing headache. I'm going to take some pills upstairs and sit quietly in that cool room until Sophie arrives.'

Max's face set. 'Of course,' he said stiffly.

'You think I'm making excuses,' she said, resigned. 'I'm not. I'd prefer to stay. Truly. But if I do I'll have a full-scale migraine, which will be no help at all for the coming showdown.'

His eyes softened. 'You look very pale, now you come to mention it,' he commented, and held out his hand. 'While we can still regard ourselves as friends, let's say our goodbyes here.'

'We don't *have* to be enemies after—afterwards, Max.'

'No, but it's more than possible there'll be sides to take, and I doubt you'll range yourself on mine,' he said grimly, and squeezed the hand she put in his.

'Thank you for driving me here,' she said huskily, her eyes locked with his. 'A pity...'

'Yes,' he agreed heavily. 'A great pity.' He raised her hand, turned it over and pressed a kiss into the palm.

Olivia felt the touch like an electric shock and pulled her hand free. She gave him a shaky little smile and turned away, her head suddenly pounding as she mounted the stairs. It seemed cowardly to let Sophie walk into the lion's den, unsuspecting, but suddenly Olivia felt a deep need to be alone. Experience had taught her that the only way to nip her headache in the bud was to wash down some pills with a copious amount of mineral water, and sit alone in her room until the dreaded phone call summoned her down to face the music. If she was honest, she admitted as she propped herself against the headboard of the bed later, the knowledge that she was unlikely to see Max Hamilton again had been partly to blame. The last few minutes with him had been such a bittersweet interlude that in the end she'd run away from him rather than spin it out any longer. Not that the headache was fiction. But a few minutes' quiet on her own would probably cure it now she'd taken the pills, whereas remaining with Max would have piled on the agony in more ways than one.

Olivia gazed from her window unseeingly, then after a while it dawned on her that she had a clear view of the car park. She slid from the bed and stood at the window to get a better view, but there was no metallic Cobra sports car amongst the others as yet. She watched absently as a scarlet Ferrari appeared through the trees and slid to a stop at the farthest point away from her. But when a slender figure jumped out of it, tossing back a mane of thick brown curls her heart gave a thump. Sophie! Olivia's hopes plummeted as she watched a tall, fair young man join her sister. So Max was right. Somewhere along the line Drew Hamilton must have exchanged his Cobra for the Ferrari. She watched as Sophie shook her head vigorously, obviously telling her companion to stay in the car while she went into the hotel. Sophie must want to speak to her big sister alone first, concluded Olivia, and turned away from the window to brush her hair gingerly, finding her head was pounding again after discovering Sophie was with Drew Hamilton after all. It was only now that she realised how passionately she'd hoped Max was mistaken.

For a moment Olivia leaned her hands on the dressing-table, eyes closed, then she jumped yards as the telephone rang, with a message from the receptionist to say Miss Collins would meet her in the annexe bar.

Olivia walked from the room on leaden feet. It seemed an interminable distance along the hushed corridors, but when she reached the stairs her pace quickened as she heard Sophie outside in the cloister bar, her voice raised in indignant counterpoint to the harsh, angry tones of Max Hamilton.

Olivia paused in the doorway, waiting for a moment as her sister faced up to Max like an angry kitten, tossing her hair back from her face.

'Mr Hamilton,' snapped Sophie, 'I have no idea where your brother is. The last time I set eyes on him was the day I left the Bellagio. He gave me a lift to the station in Venice.'

'Are you sure that's the truth, Miss Collins?' he demanded. 'Or is this a little story you and Drew cooked up between you?'

'How dare you?' stormed Sophie, her colour high. 'I hardly know Drew Hamilton.'

'So you didn't know he's about to get married?'
Sophie looked blank. 'No. Why should I?'

'Why indeed?' said Max harshly. 'It was the last thing he'd tell you if he was persuading you into a nice little holiday together.'

Sophie glared at him in outrage. 'Mr Hamilton, you have no right to talk to me like that——'

'No right at all,' said Olivia quietly, stepping out to confront them, and Sophie gave a glad cry of relief and threw herself into her sister's arms.

'Liv, this man is accusing me of running off with his brother. And I *didn't*! All I did was accept a lift to Venice to catch the train for Florence. I phoned you from there. Tell this—this Mr Hamilton I'm not lying.'

Olivia met Max's angry eyes over her sister's tumbled hair. 'Couldn't you have waited for me before you laid into Sophie like that?'

'No,' he said impatiently. 'The moment I saw her I knew she was your sister from the resemblance——'

'You mean you *know* this man?' demanded Sophie, breaking free to turn on her sister, eyes flashing.

'Yes,' said Olivia. 'Mr Hamilton came to the Bellagio looking for his brother and was told he'd left with you when you went on holiday. His brother is still missing, so Mr Hamilton assumed he was with you.'

'Well, he's *not*!' said Sophie indignantly.

'Isn't he?' asked Olivia quietly. 'I saw you arrive from my window.'

'Oh!' Sophie flushed and Max shot a questioning look at Olivia.

'Yes,' said Olivia in answer to his unspoken question. 'Sophie does have a companion——'

'And here he is,' said Sophie in sudden relief, as a tall young man with blond curly hair and blue eyes blazing in his olive-skinned face came striding towards them purposefully.

'I will wait in the car no longer, Sophie,' he said in a husky, accented voice of great charm. A voice nothing like the drawling, laid-back accents Olivia remembered from Drew Hamilton's television programme. 'You think I am *vigliacco*—afraid to meet your sister?'

Olivia looked from her radiant, smiling sister to the imperious, handsome face of the newcomer, then at Max, who was staring at the young man in obvious recognition.

'Andrea Bartoli,' he said blankly.

'Max!' The young man's face lit up as he stretched out his hand. 'What a surprise—how are you?'

Max shook the hand, looking like someone who'd just received a body blow. 'Not at my scintillating best at this particular moment in time,' he said gruffly. 'I was expecting to find Drew with Miss Sophie here.'

'Your brother?' said the boy, mystified. 'It is true I asked Drew to give Sophie a lift to the station in Venezia, but since then we have not seen him. You wish to find him?'

'I most certainly do,' said Max grimly. 'And when I do I may well murder him. One way and another he's caused me a load of trouble I could do without.'

Like meeting me? thought Olivia dully, and held out her hand to Andrea Bartoli. 'How do you do, Signor Bartoli? I'm Olivia Maitland, Sophie's sister. Do I take it you are the friend Andrea she went to Florence to meet?'

The young man flushed a little, raised Olivia's hand to his lips, then released it and put his arm round Sophie. 'I am honoured to meet you. And yes, I confess I am the friend. But we did not stay at a hotel together,' he added with a hint of hauteur. 'I took Sophie to stay at my family home, to meet my parents.'

Olivia looked questioningly at Sophie, whose expressive face bore such a mixture of triumph, happiness and guilt that it was hard to be angry with her. 'Then why all the cloak-and-dagger stuff, Sophie? At the Bellagio it seems to be the general consensus of opinion that you took off with Drew Hamilton.'

Sophie smiled proudly. 'That was a sort of smoke-screen Andrea arranged. Only Floria and Renata—the other receptionist—knew where I was really going and who I was actually going to meet.'

'Perhaps at this point, Olivia, you might like to know that the hotel is owned by the Bartoli chain,' put in Max expressionlessly. 'Andrea is the eldest Bartoli son.'

Olivia blinked. 'That's why all the secrecy, I assume?' she said, after a pause.

'*Vero*,' said Andrea simply. 'I visit all the hotels in turn to help my father. My most recent visit was to the Bellagio where I met—and fell in love with—Sophie. I wished my family to meet her before hearing any gossip from the hotel staff.' He exchanged a loving look with Sophie, then turned back to Olivia. 'When she returns to England at the end of next month I wish to travel with Sophie to meet your father, and ask his permission to marry her.'

Sophie threw herself into Olivia's arms. 'I could hardly wait for you to get here so I could tell you, but Andrea made me promise to meet his family first.'

'And do they approve?' asked Olivia, detaching herself gently. She looked very directly at Andrea Bertoli. 'How does your family feel about a marriage between their son and a foreigner employed at one of their hotels?'

'Before they met her they were doubtful,' he answered honestly. 'Even though I told them she was a student and very clever, and that one day she would be of great use to me in the business. After she has gained her degree,' he added, to clear up any doubt. 'But once they had met Sophie they had no doubts at all.'

'Not even your mother?' asked Olivia, smiling a little.

'She was a little jealous at first.' The charm of Andrea's smile told Olivia all too plainly why her sister found him irresistible. 'But not for long. Who could not love Sophie, once they had met her?'

'Look,' cut in Max brusquely, his face an expressionless mask which made him look like a stranger to Olivia, 'I'll take off at this point—leave you to your family celebration.'

'But aren't you staying here tonight?' she asked distantly, still angry with him for pouncing on Sophie so mercilessly.

'No. It's pretty pointless when Drew is obviously nowhere in the vicinity.' Max looked at her for a long moment, then turned to Sophie. 'You have my apologies, young lady. I shouldn't have jumped on you like that. My only excuse is that I'm at my wit's end as to how to find my brother.'

'Does his fiancée know he's missing?' asked Sophie with sudden sympathy.

'Yes. She's the one who asked me to look for him.'

'Oh, poor girl!' Sophie's vivid, expressive face shadowed. 'I do hope you find him soon.'

'So do I,' said Olivia coolly, and held out her hand. 'Goodbye.'

Max took it in his, holding it long enough to attract Sophie's attention. 'Goodbye, Olivia. My apologies to you, too.'

'Unnecessary,' she said distantly, removing her hand. 'Sophie was the one you bullied. Good luck with your quest.'

Max looked down at her for a moment, hesitated as though he meant to say more, then took leave of everyone and went inside the hotel.

Which, presumably, was the last she was likely to see of him, thought Olivia bleakly, as the tall, loose-limbed figure disappeared from view. She turned to the young lovers hastily, before Sophie could tune in to the unexpected feeling of loss her sister was experiencing.

CHAPTER FIVE

THE restaurant of the Villa Nerone was a very grand, formal place, with champagne provided for every diner, and a very elaborate menu.

Olivia, secretly battling with deep depression as well as her headache, did her best to hide both in an effort to keep her young companions' euphoria intact. Andrea Bartoli was a charming young man, mature for his twenty-five years, and so obviously besotted with Sophie that Olivia would have found it hard to dislike him if he'd been only a fraction as likeable. And Sophie was radiant, so incandescent with happiness that Olivia had no intention of spoiling the occasion for her by her own lack of enthusiasm for it now Max had gone.

'But how long had you known Max Hamilton?' Sophie asked once the main course was underway.

'Since Thursday,' said Olivia, conscious of enormous surprise that the time had been so brief. In some ways she felt as if she'd known Max forever.

'It was not right for him to question Sophie so alarmingly,' said Andrea in disapproval, 'but I like Max very much. He came often to the Bellagio with his family when I was a child. I used to follow him—and Drew—around like a puppy. Max taught me to swim in the pool.'

'I thought he was very overbearing,' said Sophie, sniffing. 'I was scared to death when this tall, terrifying man started firing questions about Drew at me.'

'I should have come with you as I wished,' said Andrea, frowning. 'From now on I act as I think best.'

'Oh, do you!' said Sophie challengingly, then smiled luminously, and his eyes dropped to her mouth and suddenly they were lost in a world of their own and Olivia got to her feet.

'Look, would you two mind if I went up to my room now? I have a bit of a headache. I'll leave the door on the latch, Sophie. You can let yourself in quietly when you come to bed.'

'I will not keep her late,' said Andrea, leaping to his feet. He bowed over Olivia's hand. 'I am so very glad to meet Sophie's beautiful sister at last. I hope you give us your blessing with a glad heart.'

'Would it make any difference if I didn't?' teased Olivia.

'None,' said Sophie in deadly earnest, then gave Olivia a hug. 'But I want you to be happy for me, Liv.'

'I am, love. Of course I am. By the way,' she added, 'have you rung Dad?'

'Of course I have! Andrea's spoken to him, too. So you don't have to break the glad tidings yourself,' said Sophie, smiling.

'Then I can sleep in peace tonight! Blessings, my children.' Olivia smiled at them both, then walked slowly from the dining-room, where she was bowed through the gilt and glass doors by the head waiter. It seemed a long, weary way to her room along the air-conditioned corridor, then as she unlocked her door a tall, familiar figure emerged from the neighbouring room.

'Max!' she exclaimed, startled. 'I thought you'd gone.'

'I changed my mind. I decided to stay the night after all.' He stood looking down at her in silence for a moment. 'You're as white as a sheet, Olivia. Headache still bad?'

'A bit,' she admitted. 'Where've you been?'

'I had a meal at the *trattoria* in the village. As I walked back I caught a glimpse of you in the restaurant, so I left my door open and sat watching for you.'

'I could have been hours!'

He shrugged his indifference. 'I thought you deserved to hear the glad news.'

Olivia's eyes lit up. 'You've found Drew?'

He nodded grimly. 'When I left you earlier I rang Sarah to give her the hotel number and Drew answered the phone.'

Olivia stared at him in astonishment. 'He's in *England*?'

Max nodded, his face set in harsh, angry lines. 'Lucky for him he was. If I'd been talking to him face to face I might have done him grievous bodily harm after all the trouble he's caused.'

'What happened to him?'

He took her hand. 'Look, could we go back down to the bar and talk about it?'

'I'd rather not.' Olivia felt all at sea at the sight of him. After resigning herself to never seeing Max again she found herself overwhelmed by a rush of delight so warm and unexpected that the anger she'd felt with him earlier vanished completely, taking her depression with it.

'I suppose after my attack on young Sophie you want nothing more to do with me,' he said flatly, his face settling into the harsh lines she'd begun to know so well.

'No! No, I didn't mean that!' She smiled with a warmth which brought instant response leaping into the world-weary eyes trained on her face. 'I meant I didn't fancy the bar. I can't invite you into my room,' she added diffidently. 'Sophie's sharing it with me.'

Max looked at her in silence for a long, tense moment. 'Come to mine instead,' he said gruffly at last. His smile was wry. 'I promise to behave with total circumspection.'

'Do you?' When he nodded very soberly Olivia shrugged. 'All right, but I'll have to listen for Sophie.'

'If she's with young Andrea she'll be quite a while yet.' Max ushered her into the room adjoining her own. He left the door slightly ajar, then waved her to one of the pair of armchairs which faced across a small table under the window, the same arrangement as her own room.

Olivia sat down, noting that apart from the suitcase on the luggage stand there was no sign of Max's occupation.

'Can I get you a drink?' he asked, eyeing her pallor in concern.

'Something innocuous, please.' She smiled. 'Don't keep me in suspense!'

Max found some fruit juice in his refrigerator, filled a glass for her, then poured himself a small whisky and sat facing her, his face set in grim, self-accusatory lines. 'I could have saved myself—and you and Sophie—a lot of hassle if I'd taken no notice of old Daria and rung the French number she gave me early on. I kidded myself I was sparing Luisa the worry of Drew's disappearance, but in actual fact I couldn't stomach the inevitable melodrama when Luisa heard he was missing. So I'm partly to blame for all the angst,' he added morosely, 'because my idiot brother was in France with his mother all the time. He drove there straight from dropping Sophie at the station in Venice.'

'But why didn't he get in touch with Sarah?'

'Good question! According to Drew he was finalising the details of the honeymoon he's springing on her as a surprise. After he'd sorted things out he just travelled straight back home and turned up, unheralded, on her doorstep.'

Olivia stared. 'How utterly irresponsible!'

'My sentiments exactly—only the words I used were less polite.'

'And what did Sarah do when he just appeared like that, without warning?'

Max smiled in deep satisfaction. 'She slapped the famous grin off his face, threw his ring into the street and slammed the door on him.'

'Oh, well done! But I thought you said you spoke to Drew at her place?'

'I did. Apparently he hammered on her door for ages, and made such a noise her neighbours complained and in the end she was forced to let him in.' Max scowled. 'By the time I spoke to him Drew was more subdued than I've ever heard him. I think Sarah gave him quite a fright.'

'Is the wedding still on?'

'Apparently so. Two weeks from Saturday. I hope Sarah's taught the young idiot a lesson, or I don't hold out much hope for the marriage.'

'I don't know Sarah,' said Olivia, smiling, 'but it sounds to me as if she's the ideal partner for your brother. He probably won't ever pull something so thoughtless again.'

'I hope you're right.' Max looked at her closely. 'How do you feel?'

'Better,' she said, surprised. 'My headache was bad earlier on—probably the strain of playing gooseberry all evening. Sophie and her Andrea are so much in love it's frightening.'

'You needn't worry where Andrea's concerned. He comes from splendid stock.' He smiled a little. 'And I very much doubt they're actually lovers, by the way.'

Olivia's cheeks warmed. 'I wouldn't know. I don't expect Sophie to confide in me to that extent. Though I do know she's unfashionably scornful about people who sleep around in college.'

'I know Andrea Bartoli's family well. He'll have been brought up to respect the girl he wants to marry.'

'I'm glad to hear it.' Olivia stared into her drink. 'She doesn't graduate until next summer, and I gather they don't intend marrying until then.'

'Some things are worth waiting for,' he said softly, looking at her averted face.

Olivia looked up. 'True. In one way I'm very much reassured. If they still feel the same way in a year's time at least they'll have proved it's no mere summer romance. And Sophie's still very young.'

'How old were you when you married?'

Olivia's face shadowed. 'Not much older than Sophie. But I'd only known Anthony a few weeks. Perhaps if we'd waited, got to know each other better, our marriage might have had more chance of success.'

'Do you want to talk about it?'

'No.' Olivia finished her drink. 'Time I went.'

'Don't go yet.' Max eyed her intently. 'I need to know something first. Are diplomatic relations between us irreparably severed after my run-in with Sophie this morning?'

She smiled at him sceptically. 'I'm here, in the same room with you. That should tell you something. I was furious with you at the time, but not any more.'

He gave her his sudden, transforming smile. 'Good. I count myself lucky.'

'Why?'

'That someone as beautiful as you possesses a nature as good as her looks.'

'It doesn't do to test it too far,' she warned, smiling.

'If possible I fully intend to avoid testing it ever again!' He paused. 'When do you drive to Asolo?'

'Monday morning at the crack of dawn, I suppose. It seems a fair old drive from here.'

'And when does Sophie go back to the Bellagio?'

'Tomorrow. Andrea's driving her back, he tells me, then going on to the next Bartoli hotel on his itinerary. Apparently he won't be seeing Sophie again until he joins her for the flight home to England to stay with Father.'

'So you stay here another night, then drive to Asolo for your last night.'

'That's right.' Olivia smiled at him. 'Your memory's good. How about you? Are you catching a flight back tomorrow?'

'I don't have to.' He drained his glass. 'If I make a suggestion, will you hear me out and not take flight in panic?'

'I rarely panic,' said Olivia serenely.

'You did last night.'

'That was embarrassment, not panic.'

'If you say so.' He smiled at her, then leaned forward and took her hand. 'I want to make my apologies to Sophie. I realise I must have frightened her silly. I'd like the chance to put things right with her, and with young Andrea.'

'Tonight?'

He shook his head. 'I thought perhaps you'd let me stand lunch for the three of you tomorrow to make amends.'

'I don't see why not.' She looked at him questioningly. 'What was there to panic about in that?'

'That's only half my suggestion.' His fingers tightened. 'If Andrea's driving Sophie back to the Bellagio tomorrow you'll be left on your own in the evening. I've booked in for another night. Will you spend it with me?'

'The night or the evening?' she said baldly.

Max's jaw tightened as he eyed her challengingly. 'Do you really have to ask that?'

She nodded vigorously. 'I like to get things clear before I commit myself.'

'You really got hurt, didn't you?' he said obliquely.

'Enough to make me wary, certainly.' She smiled warmly. 'But not so wary that I'll turn down company for tomorrow evening. Thank you.' She got up reluctantly. 'I'd better get back to my room before Sophie finds I'm missing and sends out a search party.'

'Don't mention the word "search" for a while,' he said, grimacing, as took her back to her room. 'If I hadn't run Drew to earth tonight the next step would have been ringing every hospital in Italy to see if he'd been admitted.'

'A good thing you were spared that!' Olivia shook her head. 'Does your brother have any idea how much worry he caused?'

'I imagine Sarah's put him right by now.' Max watched as she put her key in the door. 'Ask Sophie how she feels about lunch tomorrow when she gets in.'

'Since Andrea knows you—and approves, incidentally—I'm sure she'll accept,' Olivia assured him. 'When shall we meet up?'

'You'll want the morning to yourselves, so make it about noon in the bar downstairs. Goodnight, Olivia.' He touched a hand fleetingly to her pale cheek, then touched a finger to her bottom lip, smiling sardonically as she backed away. 'Don't worry—I wasn't optimistic enough to expect you to throw yourself into my arms after my attack on your baby sister.'

'It's not something I picture myself doing in any circumstances!'

Max looked at her for a moment, then drew her into his arms, holding her firmly as she tried to free herself. 'Since you won't throw yourself, Olivia,' he said a hairsbreadth from her mouth, 'what else can a man do?' And he stifled her protest with a kiss which put an end to her opposition.

Her response the night before had been no isolated instance, Olivia discovered, and surrendered to the exerience, forgetting caution in the simple, uncomplicated pleasure of wanting and being wanted. Because Max Hamilton made no attempt to hide the fact that he wanted her. It was implicit in the tautness of his body, the quickening of his breathing, and the deepening fervour of kisses which moved from her mouth down the long column of her throat. Olivia let out a sigh as she leaned against him, and Max raised his head and looked deep into her brilliant eyes, his breathing rapid and unsteady as he said the last thing she expected.

'Thank you, Olivia. For not fighting me off,' he added, smiling crookedly at her blank look.

'I should have done,' she said wryly, detaching herself. 'This morning I could have blacked your eye when you went for Sophie. But——' She trailed away, heat rising in her face.

'But?' he prompted softly, taking her hand.

'But now I know she's safely ensconced on a beautiful pink cloud with her Andrea I feel so relieved I don't want to murder you any more,' she said, then smiled mischievously. 'Perhaps you noticed that a moment ago.'

Max grinned. 'I don't think I did. Could you run that past me again?'

Olivia chuckled. 'Certainly not. I'm quitting while I'm ahead! Goodnight.'

As she got ready for bed she realised that her headache had mysteriously disappeared, and she felt so much better for seeing Max she could hardly believe it. After Anthony she'd always sworn she'd never let herself get close enough to a man to let one affect her life in any major way again. And there was nothing minor about Max Hamilton. His personality was abrasive, his looks striking rather than in any way handsome, but he attracted her more strongly than anyone since—since Anthony. She decided not to let the discovery worry her. After tomorrow they'd go their separate ways, probably never see each other again. Dismissing the thought quickly, she climbed into bed to watch a film on the television, until the sound of hushed voices, followed by a long silence, told her Sophie was about to join her.

When her sister stole into the room dreamy-eyed, her mouth swollen, it was obvious that a passionate embrace had been the finishing touch to her evening.

'You're awake!' exclaimed Sophie, and flung herself on the other bed, her eyes like stars. 'Did you like Andrea? Isn't he wonderful? I'm so lucky——'

'And so secretive,' put in Olivia drily. 'Why haven't I heard about him before?'

'Because I could hardly believe it was happening. I mean, the owner's son and the new receptionist! Imagine your reaction if I'd told you before you met Andrea.'

'True,' conceded Olivia, then let the tide of Sophie's confidences and plans sweep over her as her excited young sister outlined the glories of her future life as Andrea's wife. When Sophie ground to a halt at last Olivia sent her off to the bathroom to get ready for bed, waiting until the lights were out before she mentioned that she'd seen Max Hamilton again, that he'd finally tracked down his brother and wanted to take the four of them to lunch to make amends for his behaviour.

'Really?' Sophie shot up in bed and turned on her bedside light. 'Are you sure it's *me* he wants to make amends to?'

'No. He wants to make things right with Andrea, too,' said Olivia firmly.

'Then of course we'll have lunch with him.' Sophie gave her an impudent grin. 'The formidable Mr Hamilton obviously has a crush on my big sister!'

'Nonsense.' Olivia smiled, unruffled. 'Time to sleep now. No need to wish you sweet dreams, obviously.'

Sophie sighed ecstatically. 'Oh, Liv, I'm so happy.'

'Long may it last. Now please turn out your light.'

After breakfast, from which Max Hamilton was tactfully missing, the morning was spent in exploring the neighbouring village behind its fifteenth-century walls, followed by coffee back at the hotel. During the morning Andrea took pains to assure Olivia that he had no intention of diverting Sophie from her studies, since a language degree could only be an asset to the future wife of a hotelier.

'I have brothers,' he said earnestly, 'but they are younger than me, so the responsibility for the chain will eventually be mine—with their help when they are men, of course.'

Olivia smiled at him, liking Andrea Bartoli more every minute. 'And your family approves of your plans, regarding Sophie?'

'Yes,' he said simply. 'I will not lie. They were not sure before they met her.' He smiled at Sophie, who looked very young in jeans, and a T-shirt emblazoned with 'Firenze' in large letters. 'But you need have no fear, Olivia. Now they know her and have learned we are willing to wait before we marry they are truly happy for me,' he added seriously, then smiled in a way which made it all too easy for Olivia to see why her sister had fallen head over heels in love with him. 'I will find it very hard to wait——'

'So will I,' said Sophie, sighing.

'But neither of us will change in that time, even though we shall see each other very seldom,' he said, with a conviction which dispelled any last doubts Olivia might have had about their feelings for each other.

'May I join you?' said a crisp, familiar voice, and Olivia turned with a smile to greet Max Hamilton. He was casually dressed in baggy drill chinos, a yellow cotton polo shirt, with a pair of ancient deck shoes on his bare brown feet, and looked rested and, to one member of the party, at least, quite overpoweringly attractive now the haggard look of stress about him had gone.

'Max—*buona sera!*' Andrea sprang to pull out a chair. 'Olivia says you are taking us to lunch.'

Max sat down next to Olivia, but addressed himself very directly to Sophie. 'I wasn't sure you'd accept after my behaviour to this young lady yesterday. I apologise, Miss Collins. My only excuse is that I'd been so sure I'd find Drew with you, it knocked me for six when he wasn't.'

Sophie smiled, in her present mood obviously able to forgive the world. 'I quite understand. Olivia says you finally got in touch with your brother last night.'

Max nodded, and gave a dry account of Drew's reception by his fiancée. 'I don't feel I'm talking out of school,' he added, as they laughed. 'The idiot deserves a bad press after all the trouble he caused. Though,' he said, looking sideways at Olivia, 'there've been some definite compensations from my point of view.'

'You mean you would not have met Olivia otherwise,' said Andrea, grinning, and Max nodded.

'Exactly.'

'If I'm to dine here tonight,' said Olivia, changing the subject firmly, 'shall we go somewhere else for lunch? Any suggestions, Max?'

'I leave the choice to you—or to Sophie, since she's the injured party.'

'In that case, could we just go somewhere for a pizza?' said Sophie, dark eyes sparkling. 'We had such a grand dinner last night I'd like something more ordinary today.'

Max smiled at her indulgently. 'I know the very place, if Olivia will lend me her car to drive us all to Sacile.'

'Sacile?' repeated Olivia, as she strolled beside him to the car park later. 'Isn't that your stepmother's home?'

'I wouldn't suggest it if she were in town,' he said sardonically, then smiled. 'At the Ristorante Cellini all you get is pizza, by the way, so if you fancy something different now's the time to back out.'

'I can hardly come to Italy and not eat pizza,' she said, shrugging, secretly not caring what they ate. It was a beautiful day, she was now sure all was well with Sophie, Max had solved the mystery of his brother's disappearance, and when Sophie and her Andrea left later this afternoon there was the evening with Max to look forward to. For the moment all was remarkably right with her world.

Sacile was a pretty little town. As they passed a particularly beautiful house, with rose coloured walls, and geraniums trailing from its balconies Max waved a hand at it.

'Luisa's place,' he said briefly. 'You remember Drew's mother, Andrea?' he added, raising his voice.

'Very well,' said the young man warmly. 'How is the beautiful Signora Hamilton?'

'She doesn't change much,' said Max drily as he parked neatly in the last free place in a piazza watched over by the tall campanile of the local church.

'Why are the bell towers separate in this part of the world?' asked Olivia curiously as the four of them strolled to the nearby restaurant.

Andrea shrugged. 'It is a feature of our architecture. Some of them were used in times of war, also, as lookouts to watch for the enemy.'

The Cellini was a busy, well patronised place with a large main dining-room encircled outside by a veranda with trailing greenery and more geraniums, where they were given a table which looked out on the piazza.

The menus gave them three pages of variations to choose from and Sophie went through every one twice over before deciding on tuna, asparagus and pepper.

'What does San Daniele mean?' inquired Olivia.

'It is the local *prosciutto crudo*, and very good,' said Andrea.

'You order that,' said Max, 'I'll take the artichoke and we'll go halves.'

'Done!' said Olivia, while Sophie teased Andrea about his conventional choice of ham and mushroom.

'Ah, but the mushrooms are the first of the *porcini* he said reverently, and Olivia laughed, describing her abortive efforts to avoid a first course at Harry's Bar.

'Goodness,' said Sophie, round-eyed, 'does your firm rise to places like that for your research?'

'Actually Max was kind enough to treat me to lunch there.'

'In return for a lift to Pordenone in the car she'd hired,' said Max matter-of-factly.

Sophie blinked, giving Olivia a look which meant 'I'll talk to you later in private', then buttered one of the crisp, delicious rolls which seemed to come with everything in this part of the world. 'Mmm, I'm starving,' she said, mouth full, and Andrea laughed.

'Such enthusiasm for food is not very romantic, *carissima.*'

'Nothing turns me off my food—not even love,' she retorted cheerfully.

The meal was a lively, protracted affair, the pizzas delicious and a far cry from lesser varieties Olivia had sampled outside Italy. It was well into the afternoon before they got back to the Nerone, leaving Sophie very little time alone with Olivia when they went to their room.

'You didn't say you spent the day in Venice with Max!' she said, stuffing her belongings into an overnight bag. 'I thought he was searching high and low for his brother, not swanning off with my sister.'

'He was convinced Drew was with you,' Olivia reminded her. 'So with time to kill until yesterday he offered to act as my guide.'

Sophie slung the strap of her bag over her shoulder and frowned at her sister. 'Do you like him, Liv?'

'Yes,' said Olivia casually, and shooed her sister from the room. 'Come on, or we'll have Andrea galloping up here to see what's taking you so long.'

'And you do like Andrea—I mean *really*?' said Sophie, as they hurried along the air-conditioned corridor.

'He's a charmer, and it's obvious he adores you, so how could I help it?' Olivia gave her sister a hug. 'And not many men would be patient enough to wait for a year to have you.'

'How do you know that?' queried Sophie, blushing scarlet.

'I meant until he married you.'

'Oh.' Sophie smiled sheepishly. 'Well in case you were wondering, we haven't, I mean we're not sleeping together until then.'

'I wasn't wondering,' said Olivia quietly, 'because that's entirely your business, but since you're obviously so mad about each other Andrea must be a pretty strong character to agree to wait.'

Sophie pulled a face. 'I know it sounds a bit medieval, and in college people would laugh themselves silly if they knew——'

'Why should they know?' said Olivia, and patted Sophie's cheek.

'Did you? Before you and Anthony were married, I mean?'

'No.'

Sophie nodded triumphantly. 'I thought not. If you could hold out, so can we!'

CHAPTER SIX

'You seem rather pensive this evening,' said Max later, in the lively trattoria in the village. 'Are you sure you wouldn't have preferred the splendours of the Nerone dining room?'

'Definitely not,' said Olivia firmly, and smiled. 'This is much more fun. Besides, it gives me more information to report to my clients.'

'You think many people would choose this particular place for a holiday?'

'Not an entire holiday, but certainly a stopover like this on a tour of the Veneto.'

'Which doesn't give me the reason for the shadows under those remarkable eyes,' he persisted. 'Was it a wrench to part with Sophie?'

'No, not really. I'll be seeing her again soon enough. And now I've met Andrea I think I'll have to get used to seeing a lot less of my little sister anyway. If things turn out as they plan, her life will be spent entirely in this country once she's married.'

'Will you mind that?'

Olivia met his eyes squarely. 'If it means she'll lead a happy, fulfilled life I shan't mind in the slightest.'

'Does she know your marriage wasn't a success?'

'I hope not. She rarely came to stay when I was married to Anthony, and our trips to Cheltenham were generally for Christmas, or birthday celebrations, times when it was easy to conceal the lack of connubial bliss in the Maitland household.'

Max leaned back in his chair after their plates were removed, studying her intently. 'Did you work in your present job when you were married?'

'Oh, yes, but I was a mere underling in those days. I only reached my present giddy heights after Anthony—died.' She drank some water quickly. 'It's a very interesting job, actually. I put together itineraries tailor-made for individual clients in every detail. People ring up with no prior knowledge of whatever area it is they fancy visiting, and often it's down to me to plan their entire holiday. It's a responsibility I take very seriously.'

'Is all this done over the phone?'

'Mostly, yes. Some days I don't get down to the actual paperwork until after five or so, which means staying as late as seven, or even eight in the evening to get it down.' She smiled at him. 'I sound like a right Goody Two Shoes, but it really does matter to me to make my clients' holidays as perfect as possible.'

Max frowned. 'You sound as though it's your life.'

She shook her head. 'Once I get home I switch off, leave the job behind. I'm one of those people who can keep their life in separate compartments, fortunately—a knack I developed early on.'

'To keep your work from spilling over into your private life?'

'No. The other way round.'

The night was overcast as they walked slowly back through the village later, past cafés where people sat at tables outside in the heat, talking the evening away.

'Could be in for a storm,' commented Max. 'Even I feel the heat tonight. Do you mind storms?'

'I'm not mad about them if I'm outside, but indoors I'm all right.'

He took her hand. 'You can always knock on my door if you're frightened.'

'I wouldn't dream of disturbing your beauty sleep,' she said lightly. 'If the worst comes to the worst I'll shut myself in the bathroom and read until it's over.'

Max halted as they came to the gates leading into the gardens of the Nerone. 'Olivia, before we go in I've got something to say.'

She stiffened, eyeing him warily.

'I won't beat about the bush,' he said quickly. 'The last thing I want is to fly back to England tomorrow while you go on alone to Asolo.' His hand tightened on hers. 'It's a fair trip by car. I know the road fairly well and the Villa Cipriani can fit me in tomorrow night. Let me drive you to Asolo.'

Olivia eyed him in silence, clamping down on a sudden rush of excitement. 'When did you ring the Cipriani?'

'This morning, before breakfast.'

'And you haven't mentioned it until now!'

He shook his head, his teeth showing white in a crooked smile. 'I was biding my time. It seemed prudent to make my apologies, then behave so impeccably all day that I would have atoned for the scene with Sophie before I brought the subject up.'

'So the lunch and this evening were all a softening up process to get your own way,' said Olivia, as they resumed walking.

'Not at all. I was taking your advice.'

'*My* advice?'

'On the use of tact.'

Olivia chuckled reluctantly, deeply pleased by his suggestion, but determined not to jump at it too eagerly. 'I'm a perfectly capable driver,' she informed him drily. 'A two-hour journey to Asolo is quite within my powers.'

'I disapprove of women driving alone in foreign countries,' he announced with deliberate provocation.

'Sexist.'

'Perhaps I should have said a woman as beautiful as you,' he amended.

'That's even worse!'

'Let's have a drink here while we finish the argument,' Max suggested, as they reached the deserted cloister bar. 'It's too hot to go indoors yet.'

'Our rooms are air-conditioned,' she pointed out.

'Air-conditioning's no exchange for your company,' he assured her. 'What would you like?'

'It's the wrong time of day to ask for tea, I suppose?'

Max gave the order in rapid Italian to the waiter, then shook his head at her in mock reproof.

'Essential to report on the tea supply for your British clients, Olivia. If you want something, ask for it.'

'Is that your own personal motto for life?' she retorted.

He met her eyes levelly. 'Not up to now. I've tended to take what I wanted more often than not. But since meeting you I've learnt my lesson.'

'What lesson is that?'

'If the object desired is sublime enough it's worth taking whatever time and trouble is necessary to secure it.'

'Would you care to define the word ''object''?' she asked thoughtfully.

'I'm speaking in the abstract.' Max paused to allow the waiter to place all the makings for Olivia's tea in front of her, waiting until his glass of beer arrived and they were safe from interruption before he continued. 'You obviously harbour dark suspicions about my motives for wanting to see more of you.'

'Perfectly natural,' she observed evenly, and poured hot water on to her English Breakfast teabag.

Max leaned his arms on the table and gazed deep into her eyes. 'If you expect me to say I don't want you physically, Olivia, you'll be disappointed. I'm not lacking in the usual arrangement of male hormones, and you are the exact personification of what I'm drawn to most in a woman: intelligence, maturity, and with a withdrawn, private quality to your looks I find totally irresistible. But strange as it may seem I want your friendship and your company, as well as the obvious, and as I know damn well any misguided urge to stampede you into bed would lose me both I promise I won't try anything so stupid—you have my word.'

She stared back, fascinated. 'That's—that's a fairly comprehensive statement.'

'So what's your answer?'

'What will you do if I say no?'

'Hire a car in the morning, drive back to Venice and get on the first available flight to Heathrow.'

Olivia hesitated, then shrugged. 'Since you've gone to the trouble of booking a room at the Villa Cipriani it seems a shame to waste it. And I'd be foolish to turn down the services of an expert guide and driver. If you really would like to come, why not?'

Max's eyes narrowed through his thick black lashes. 'You enjoyed letting me stew there for a while, I assume?'

'You bet,' she admitted cheerfully, and treated herself to a second teabag. 'If you've been used to getting what you want without even asking, a little stewing might be just what you need.'

He chuckled. 'You may be right.'

'That's settled then,' she said briskly. 'My plan was to set out early, so shall we meet at the car at eight?'

The drive to Asolo next day was accomplished smoothly, with no hold-ups in traffic, and rarely a break in conversation. Freed from the burden of finding his missing brother, Max Hamilton was a very entertaining companion as he recounted some of his adventures on his travels round the world.

'And how about you?' said Max. 'With all the expert advice you give to your clients, what's your idea of the perfect holiday?'

'My idea of heaven is a weekend in one of those luxurious country house hotels with roaring fires and four-poster beds, and nothing more energetic than a walk in the grounds before dinner,' said Olivia pensively. 'Though this part of the world takes some beating. I see we're beginning to climb. Isn't Asolo at the foot of the Grappa mountains?'

'Yes—we're almost there. Incidentally, some of the streets are so narrow we'll have to wait at traffic lights to get into the town to start with,' he told her.

As the tree-lined road curved upward from the plain, swooping up towards the town, Olivia was more glad than ever that Max had elected to come with her. 'I haven't driven on the right enough to be completely comfortable,' she admitted, and sent a smile in his direction. 'I'm glad you volunteered, Max.'

He glanced sideways for a fleeting instant, a gleam in his dark eyes. 'For a moment last night I thought you were going to refuse my offer.'

'It never does to look too eager,' she said demurely, then exclaimed in delight as the town appeared on the hillside above them in a series of cinnamon roofs and pale walls, interspersed with greenery and tall, pointing fingers of cypress, surmounted by a hill topped with a ruined fortress.

'That's the Rocca,' said Max as they entered the town to wait at a red light. 'It's a ruined fortification that predates even Roman times, apparently.'

Olivia looked about her eagerly as they drove through the town, where to her surprise no modern buildings appeared among the mainly Venetian-influenced architecture. They passed the main piazza, where a fountain topped by the lion of Venice provided the focal point of a busy square which could have come straight out of one of Goldoni's plays. It was a bustling place, lined with shops and cafés and bright with colour from the flowers trailing from balconies and window boxes.

Max smiled at her enthusiasm as he negotiated a street which narrowed alarmingly as it led under an arch formed by a wing of a large, green-shuttered house with walls the colour of terracotta. And suddenly they were at the Villa Cipriani, which, unlike either of the two previous hotels, had its main entrance on the street, with its gardens behind it, hidden from view. As Max halted the car, eyeing the tricky entrance of the hotel garage on the opposite side of the road, a young man hurried from the hotel to park the car and bring their luggage.

Olivia stood for a moment, gazing up at the villa's façade, which was broken by an irregular arrangement of green-shuttered windows, some in pairs, others single, and in one instance on the second floor a trio grouped together with a balcony. Then she hurried quickly after Max, who was announcing their arrival to a suave young man behind the reception desk. The latter welcomed them in perfect English, asked them if they were dining that evening, then clicked his fingers imperiously once they'd signed in and told a porter to conduct them to their rooms. They left the porter to take up the luggage in the small lift, and went in search of their rooms together, only too glad to walk up the shallow, red-carpeted stairs after the car journey. Max's room was on the first floor, but Olivia, smiling, declined the offer of his escort to the next floor.

'I'll see you downstairs in half an hour,' she said and went on to meet the porter with her luggage outside her room, delighted when she realised that the spacious bedroom was the one she'd seen from outside. It not only boasted a balcony with triple windows looking down on the street outside, but gave her a view of the very photogenic garden from another pair of tall, shuttered windows on the adjoining wall. Olivia gazed around the room, deeply impressed. The beds were each wide enough to take two people at a pinch, there was a huge, mirror-backed mahogany sideboard, with plates of fresh fruit and a tall vase of scarlet gladioli. A sofa and two chairs were grouped about a low table piled with glossy magazines, and alongside a vast mahogany wardrobe a door opened into a bathroom lined with vivid floral tiles.

This, thought Olivia, freshening up in the bathroom rapidly, was old-established luxury, discreetly palatial. And the villa had such heavenly views of cypress-crowned hills from its windows that it was no wonder Robert Browning had been so inspired by the place.

She changed into her striped skirt and long silk sweater, made a few deft touches to her face and hair, then went in search of Max.

He was reading a paper in the foyer, and rose quickly as Olivia came running down the stairs. 'You look good. What's the programme for the rest of the day?'

Olivia smiled. 'What I really want is just a stroll round the town, then a table at one of the outdoor cafés in the square to watch the world go by and soak up the local atmosphere.'

'Sounds good to me,' he agreed. 'You're sure you don't want me to drive you to explore the beauties of the *campagna* first?'

'I get a quite remarkable view of some of the local countryside from my bedroom window, thanks just the same. And it's a pity to waste this sunshine sitting in the car. By the way, there was no storm last night after all.'

'I heard a few rumbles, but it must have missed Pordenone.' He steered her across the narrow street and on to a cobbled pavement which rose so steeply there were handrails for the fainthearted. The pavement took them under a colonnade of arches, where tempting shop windows made progress slow. It came to a complete standstill when Olivia found a shop displaying water-colours of various parts of Asolo.

'I'd love one of these!' she exclaimed, peering through the glass.

'Want me to make a deal on one for you?'

Half an hour later Olivia was the owner of an exquisite little water-colour of the fountain in the piazza, sold to her by the artist herself.

'Such a shy, sweet woman,' said Olivia later. 'I hope you didn't beat her down too much.'

'We merely came to a happy compromise about the frame,' he assured her, then led her away towards the piazza, and lunch. 'Come on. It's a long time since breakfast. I need refuelling.'

They found an empty table with an umbrella to shield them from the noonday sun, and ordered plates of gnocchi with tomato sauce and a bottle of light, sparkling wine Olivia agreed to share for once. Utterly relaxed, some of her habitual reserve lessened, and she found herself talking to Max as though she'd known him for years instead of days, reading out bits from the guide-book he'd bought her to learn the history of the town.

'It says Browning broke all known rules of Italian grammar by calling his last, unfinished poem "Asolando",' she informed Max. 'But he also wrote his first poem, "Pippa Passes" here too. He must have been big in Asolo—they even named a street after him.'

'Quite a few literati were drawn to the place—one of them called it the town of a hundred horizons. But Browning was pretty sold on most of Italy. He lived with his Elizabeth in Florence for years.'

Olivia sighed. 'Their story seems so romantic: Elizabeth a chronic invalid for years, then Robert Browning sweeping into her existence like some life-giving force, practically kidnapping her to carry her off to Italy.' Her eyes shone green under the shade of the umbrella. 'Do you suppose they were really happy ever after together?'

'I doubt it. Not all the time, certainly. They were both human beings so I imagine they had their ups and downs, and had to work to make their marriage a success, just like anyone else brave enough to embark on matrimony——' Max halted as he saw the change in Olivia's face and cursed softly under his breath. 'Hell, Olivia, I'm sorry. My famous lack of tact again. I wasn't denigrating your own efforts at marriage, I swear.'

'No, I know,' she returned matter-of-factly. 'But you're right, just the same. A happy marriage isn't something you get handed on a plate. It's the result of give and take and compromise and a great many things mine didn't have going for it.' She smiled at him resolutely. 'Let's talk about something else.'

'What shall we do after lunch?' he said promptly. 'Churches? More shops? After which you'll probably need a rest in your room before we sample the offerings of the Cipriani kitchens this evening.'

As they strolled together through the town, admiring the Venetian-style architecture and abundance of romanesque windows, Olivia knew she was finding more pleasure in everything with Max for company than she'd have done on her own. They browsed in antique shops whose interiors backed on to walls formed by the great rock of the hill overshadowing the town, then strolled to the parish church, Santa Maria di Breda, which was a large basilica full of valuable paintings, and proud of its claim to have been the diocesan centre of the area even before the year 1000.

'There's such a sense of timelessness in this place,' whispered Olivia, as they made their way outside to find the sunshine had taken on a darkly metallic sheen.

'And pretty soon we're going to be drenched,' said Max prosaically, as a rumble of thunder sounded too close for comfort. 'Come on—let's make a run for it.'

But by the time they reached the main piazza the sky was ominously black and the rain was pouring down. As they slithered across the streaming cobbles there was a sizzle as lightning struck almost at their feet, with a simultaneous crack of thunder loud enough to make their eardrums ring. Olivia gave a screech of panic and flew across the square and into one of the cafés, Max hard on her heels.

'Could we stay for a while?' she panted, white-faced. 'That was a bit too close for comfort!'

'Stay as long as you like,' he said, pulling out a chair for her. 'Here. Sit with your back to the door so you don't see the lightning. I'll order tea for you.'

Olivia smiled at him gratefully, her heart beating like a drum as she dabbed at hair sleeked to her head by the downpour.

'Do these storms go on for long?' she added, wincing as thunder crashed again when Max joined her.

'I shouldn't think so.' He waved a hand at the proprietor, who was busy taking his potted plants outside to catch the rain. 'At least it saves *him* a job tonight.'

Olivia smiled, feeling better. 'Sorry to be so feeble, but a fork of lightning right at my feet was a bit over the top!'

Max smiled, and leaned to retrieve a newspaper from one of the adjoining tables as the lady of the establishment served them with the now familiar pots of hot water and lemon slices, but this time they came with a small pitcher of cold milk, and the teabags were Earl Grey.

'Obviously used to British customers,' commented Olivia.

'There are quite a few expatriate Brits living in these parts,' he told her, 'mainly wealthy ones, at a guess.'

Olivia nodded. 'The prices in some of the shops were astronomical. But it's such a beautiful place that I can quite understand anyone wanting to settle here.'

'Would you like to make your home outside Britain?' he asked curiously.

She shook her head. 'I don't think so. It's different for Sophie, of course.'

'Why?'

'Because she's so much in love with Andrea I don't think she cares where she lives as long as it's with him!'

'And is falling in love something you consider unlikely where you're concerned?'

'I've done it once—which was more than enough.'

Max looked at her in silence for a moment. 'Seems a waste,' he observed eventually.

'Why should living my life without a man in it be some kind of waste?' she parried. 'Is *your* life considered a waste for the same reason? No woman in it, I mean?'

'I've never thought about it,' he said, off-hand, and leaned forward. 'What I meant, Olivia, is that you would make some man a wonderful wife, and in natural progression, an equally wonderful mother.'

'I prefer things the way they are,' she said, but with a conviction she found she had to work at under the analytical gaze which seemed to see right through the smokescreen she was putting up.

For years she'd had her life arranged in exactly the way she wanted it, with no man to interfere in her serene, well-ordered existence, her home and her bed completely free of any male intrusion. Now, after only a few short days in Max's company, the arrangement seemed arid and incomplete, a discovery which left her shaken. To find herself thinking about wedding bells and the patter of tiny feet after a mere few days of acquaintance with a man was sheer lunacy. She'd rushed into marriage with Anthony, and the end result of that should have served as a very clear warning about ever entering into something similar again. But the fact remained that she wasn't looking forward to saying goodbye to Max when they reached England. She looked up at him suddenly as it occurred to her she'd never asked where he lived.

'When you said you intended to be UK based from now on, what part of the country did you mean?'

'The head office is in Kew,' he answered, smiling a little. 'Why? Were you hoping for Land's End, or the Outer Hebrides?'

Olivia poured herself more tea, chuckling. 'No, of course not.'

'I live in Kew, not far from the firm. Drew, by the way, is based in Birmingham, where the programme comes from. He's bought a house in Edgbaston. Sarah's starting a new teaching job there in September.'

'She's a teacher?' Olivia smiled, surprised. 'I thought someone like Drew would have gone for a model, or someone in showbusiness.'

'He has done in the past. Then he met Sarah again. Her family lived near us when we were young, but they moved away to Gloucestershire when she was twelve or so. She met up with Drew by chance at a wedding last year, by which time the roly poly with plaits had metamorphosed into a willowy girl with the sort of quiet good looks that knock spots off the surface glamour Drew's usually drawn to. One look and he was bowled over.'

'Sarah likewise?'

'No.' Max smiled rather smugly. 'His playboy image did him no favours where she was concerned. I believe it took a lot of pretty intensive courtship on his part to change her mind.'

'Sarah sounds like exactly the right partner for him,' said Olivia. 'I hope they'll be very happy.'

Max looked at her for a moment. 'Olivia,' he said slowly, 'if I get Sarah to send you an invitation, will you come to the wedding? With me, as my guest?'

She stared at him in astonishment. 'But your family won't want strangers at the wedding, even if——'

'Even if you had any intention of saying yes,' he said sardonically. 'Forget it. I asked on impulse. Shall we make a move? The thunder's passed over, though it's still raining cats and dogs.'

'I'm not afraid of rain,' she assured him, rather nettled by his curt reaction to her token protest.

As they hurried the short, deeply descending distance to the hotel Olivia found the wet cobbles hard going, and was forced to accept a helping hand from

Max, annoyed by her leap of response as his warm hand steadied hers.

'You're annoyed because I didn't jump at the invitation,' she said bluntly, as they waited for a break in the traffic to cross the road.

'No. Just irritated for making such a damn-fool suggestion,' he said shortly, and took her by the arm to run with her across the narrow street, and into the hotel, making further conversation on the subject impossible, as the hotel manager greeted them with suave apologies for the weather in Asolo.

'I'll see you about seven-thirty for a drink,' said Max, as they paused at the first landing.

'Right.' Olivia eyed him uncertainly, but something in his expression warned her against any further comment on the wedding invitation, and she ran lightly up the next flight of stairs without a backward glance.

After a long soak in scented water, followed by a vigorous session with shampoo and hairdrier, Olivia lay on the wonderfully comfortable bed with a book she hardly glanced at as she watched the sky clear from the windows looking out over the garden. The smell of wet grass and flowers came up to her, rich and heady in the warm evening air, and she slid off the bed to lean at the window, looking out over a view of campaniles and green hills, with pale buildings glimmering here and there in a landscape as beautiful and changeless as a painting by an old master.

She leaned at the window to admire it, wondering if she should have accepted the wedding invitation after all. She disliked the thought of parting with Max tomorrow, though the fact that he worked in London seemed to indicate the parting might not be permanent. If he should want to explore their relationship further it was at least geographically possible. Perhaps, over dinner, she could bring the subject up casually, indicate that although the wedding idea wasn't something she fancied very much, it needn't rule further contact between them. If only the wretched man wasn't so touchy! In which case, of course, it might be better not to promote any further meetings between them at all. Max Hamilton was the wrong man to spend time with if her aim was to keep her life serene and undisturbed. His lovemaking the night before had been proof of that, if she'd needed any. Brief though it was, it had been an exciting, illuminating experience, teaching her that reactions she'd believed dead and buried forever were alive and flourishing after all. The problem, of course, was that kissing wasn't a static pastime. It inevitably led to other things, as it was designed to do, and she wasn't prepared for that yet. If she ever would be. Anthony, one way and another, had seen to that.

CHAPTER SEVEN

AT SEVEN-THIRTY on the dot, wearing a dress as understated as a T-shirt in muted rose crêpe, her only touches of green her peridot ear-studs and the eyes she'd accented with rather more drama than usual, Olivia went slowly down the wide, shallow stairs to the foyer, past the signed photograph of the Queen Mother on the wall, and found that Max was nowhere in sight. Unwilling to sit in the crowded bar alone, she wandered outside in the garden, along paths made of pale stepping-stones raying from a central point formed by a very picturesque well. From this angle she realised the villa and its garden were on the summit of a hill, and from a hibiscus hedge at the end of the lawn, other terraced levels of gardens fell away in tiers below, every flower and blade of glass glittering as sunlight on raindrops gave a bejewelled look to the landscape.

'It is very beautiful, is it not?' said a husky male voice, and Olivia turned to find a man watching her, a smile in his dark blue eyes. He was faultlessly dressed in a well-groomed, casual way, and spoke with an attractive trace of accent.

'Very beautiful,' agreed Olivia. 'It's such a lovely evening after that terrible storm this afternoon.'

He chuckled. 'You must be English!'

She smiled involuntarily. 'Because I mentioned the weather?'

'Of course. Also many English people visit the Villa Cipriani.'

'Including our poet, Robert Browning.'

'*Esattamente.*' He smiled, the blue eyes gleaming. 'But in his day it was not a hotel, but his home for a time.'

'The perfect place for a poet,' she agreed.

'You are here on holiday?' asked the urbane stranger.

'Only for tonight,' she said with regret.

'You are alone?'

'There you are, Olivia,' interrupted a brusque voice, and a hard hand clasped hers, pointedly proprietorial.

She glanced up at Max, who looked just as elegant as the stranger in the suit he'd worn at the Bellagio. 'You're late,' she said coolly. 'This gentleman and I were just commenting on the beauty of the evening.'

Max nodded distantly to the Italian, who smiled at Olivia, gave Max the faintest of ironic bows and strolled away across the garden.

'Who the hell was that?' he demanded.

Olivia pulled free. 'How should I know? One of the other guests, I suppose.'

'He was trying to chat you up!'

'He scarcely spoke two words to me,' she retorted crossly.

'He was watching you for some time before that. I saw him from my window.'

'If you'd been on time, *instead* of watching from your window, he wouldn't have had the chance to speak to me!' She turned away to stare at the view, rubbing her wrist where his fingers had marked the skin. 'At least his approach, whoever he is, had a lot more going for it than yours, as I remember it.'

'I'm bloody sure it did. Probably thought he was on to a good thing.'

'Rubbish!' Olivia turned on him, eyes flashing like an angry tigress. 'Besides, who I choose to speak to is my business.'

'Surely you realise you're asking for trouble if you encourage all and sundry on these solo trips of yours?' he demanded furiously.

'As I did in your case, you mean!'

'Hell, no——' He stopped, thrust a hand through his overlong hair and breathed in deeply. 'Why the devil are we fighting?'

'You are fighting. *I* am not,' said Olivia succinctly.

He eyed her blankly, calming down. 'I suppose I was jealous,' he said slowly, so patently astonished by the discovery that she had to bite back a laugh.

'Not that you've any right to it, or any cause,' she said carefully, 'but why is jealousy such a surprise?'

'It took me a while to recognise the emotion. It's not one I'm familiar with.'

She smiled faintly. 'Neither am I. But don't worry. Where I'm concerned it's not one likely to trouble you much in future.'

'Meaning that you promise not to give me cause?' he enquired conversationally.

Olivia's eyes flashed. 'Meaning,' she repeated deliberately, 'that we go our separate ways as from tomorrow.'

Max, in command of himself again, gave her an irritatingly indulgent smile. 'If you really believe that, Olivia Maitland, you've far less intelligence than I credited you with. You know damn well I'm attracted to you, I enjoy your company, and I'm pretty sure you enjoy mine, otherwise you'd never have agreed to it today. Can you give me one good reason why we shouldn't go on seeing each other once we get back?'

'If that's how you feel, why were you so angry when I turned down the wedding idea?' she demanded.

'I tend to expect people to fall in with my suggestions,' he admitted, shrugging.

'You mean orders!'

He grinned, disarming her. 'Look. The wedding—let's start again. I'm not best man—not even an usher. I declined the honour, far preferring to take a back seat and leave the limelight to Sarah and Drew. To be blunt, I detest weddings, but if you came with me it would make the day a hell of a sight more enjoyable from my point of view. It's in a little village near Cheltenham by the way, which means you could stay with your father——'

'Whoa!' said Olivia, thawing. 'Even if I said yes—which I haven't,' she added hastily, at his look of triumph, 'how would you explain my presence at such a private sort of family occasion?'

'I've already told Drew what happened. How his idiotic behaviour nearly cost me the chance of getting to know the most beautiful woman I've ever met,' he said casually.

Olivia looked at him without expression. 'But that's just the point. You don't know me.'

'And never will,' he retorted impatiently, 'unless you co-operate.'

'Your chat-up line could do with some work,' she told him, shaking her head. 'Let's have a pre-dinner drink and declare a truce. If you go on glowering at me like that I'll get indigestion.'

He laughed, and took her hand, more gently this time, as they strolled towards the bar. As their fingers linked the simple contact suddenly gave the evening a different quality, both of them deeply aware that this was their last evening in Italy, and whatever the future might or might not hold, this was a special occasion. Even the sight of the urbane, blue-eyed stranger seated alone at one of the dining tables failed to dispel the magic Olivia knew Max felt as strongly as she did. As they nibbled the crisp deep-fried courgette flowers they were given for appetisers, Max's mood improved to the point where he was able to tease her about the presence of her admirer.

'If I were called away suddenly, you wouldn't lack company for long,' he remarked, grinning.

'Wouldn't I have any say in that?' she retorted.

'You looked quite happy to talk to the guy earlier!'

'He was charming,' she agreed.

'Unlike me, you mean.'

Olivia looked assessingly into the hard, assertive face so close to her own. 'Of all the words to describe you I admit "charming" isn't the first to leap to mind.'

'Is that what you value most in a man—charm?'

She shook her head. 'Least, probably.'

'Glad to hear it. I'm a pretty straightforward sort of a guy.' He leaned nearer, looking deep into her eyes. 'I'm warning you now. I don't intend to let you get away.'

Olivia stared at him, arrested, her pulse racing and colour rushing to her face so suddenly that for once it was plainly visible.

'You're blushing,' he said very quietly.

'It doesn't usually show,' she muttered, embarrassed.

'Don't worry. Only I can tell.' His eyes lit with a molten gleam. 'Incredible. Like red wine spilled in a bowl of cream.'

Olivia gave him a fulminating glance. 'Will you please stop discussing it?'

'Why did you blush?' he demanded relentlessly.

'You're very forthright, Mr Hamilton.'

'I'm famous for it,' he agreed blandly.

Olivia looked blank as the waiter placed a dish of some creamy confection in front of her.

'Did I order this?' she asked Max, eyeing it in surprise.

'No, I did. This is the region where the now common tiramisu originated. I felt you were obliged to sample it, if only in the course of duty.' His eyes danced as they held hers, and Olivia smiled back, her eyes giving off green sparks in the candlelight.

'Duty doesn't usually present itself in such agreeable form,' she said happily, then went into raptures as she tasted the first spoonful. 'Wonderful!'

After the meal they went for a stroll in the garden and stood gazing out over the moonlit *campagna* as they discussed the timetable for the next day.

'I managed to book a seat on your flight,' said Max. 'So unless we fall out irredeemably between here and Marco Polo we can journey together all the way. Is someone meeting you at Heathrow?'

Olivia shook her head. 'I'll probably splash out on a taxi instead of struggling with the tube.'

'I'll share it with you—if I may,' he added belatedly.

'Since you actually remembered to ask so nicely, how can I refuse?' she teased.

'I spend too much time in the company of my own sex, subordinates at that,' he said wryly. 'Finesse isn't something I need much in my line of work.'

'I think I like that,' she said consideringly, and smiled up at him.

Max moved closer and took her hand in his. 'Let's take a stroll round the town. It's too early to go in yet.'

They left the hotel to wander through the softly lit streets, the moon adding an other-worldly quality to a town which at night looked as though the centuries had barely touched it. When Max took her arm to cross the narrow street at the hotel he kept it linked through his, holding her close to his side, the proximity filling Olivia with a excitement and something else she finally identified as anticipation.

Anticipation of what? she asked herself. Max had been honest about finding her physically attractive, but equally positive about refraining from doing anything drastic about it in case it lost him her company.

'You're very quiet,' observed Max, as they paused at the balustrade near the flight of steps leading down from the basilica.

'I was daydreaming, if one can call it that at this time of night.' She smiled up at him, her eyes dark in a face washed pale by the moon. 'Odd really. We met such a short time ago, and yet in some ways I feel I've known you a lot longer than a few days.'

'Perhaps it was our shared stress over Sophie and Drew.' Max smiled. 'And since we're such old friends on such short acquaintance, I insist you come to Drew's wedding with me. It's only fair.'

'Fair?'

'You were with me on the hunt for him. It seems only fitting you should be in at the death.'

Olivia frowned at him in assumed disapproval. 'I'm not much sold on the institution of marriage, I admit, but it's a bit much to refer to it as death!'

Max took her hand in his, brushing her words aside. 'Come with me, Olivia. It won't even take up your whole day. The bride and groom are leaving immediately once they've cut the cake, for a honeymoon in France. Which, remember, was the reason for Drew's visit to his mother there and the cause of all the trouble. He was making certain arrangements Sarah doesn't know about.'

'Do you?' asked Olivia, intrigued.

'I believe they involve the bridal suite in a château, and champagne and roses and every last touch my brother could think of to charm his new wife,' said Max softly. 'For once he has my entire approval. Sarah deserves it.'

'The way you talk about her one might almost think you envy your brother his bride,' said Olivia without thinking, then gasped as Max pulled her suddenly into his arms and held her there as he stared down into her face.

'You couldn't be more wrong! I'm holding the contradiction to your theory right here in my arms,' he added, in a tone which quickened her heartbeat.

Olivia pushed against him. 'Max, for heaven's sake, we're in a public place!'

'Then let's find a more private one,' he said swiftly, and dropped his arms to take her hand.

They walked back through the town to the hotel in silence, so physically aware of each other that Olivia's nerves jangled as his fingers closed on hers to bring her close beside him again as they walked. Unable to bear it, she burst into conversation as they left the piazza for the street leading to the hotel.

'The large pink house just before the Villa Cipriani,' she said in desperation. 'Who lives there?'

'It once belonged to Eleanora Duse,' said Max, an indulgent note in his voice. 'She was Italy's equivalent to France's Sarah Bernhardt, and a far more talented actress, according to George Bernard Shaw. She was a sad sort of person who found a little happiness in Asolo, so she asked to be buried here.'

'I can understand why,' said Olivia, then shivered suddenly, and Max's grasp tightened on her hand.

'Come on, you need cheering up,' he said firmly, and held the hotel door open for her. 'Would you like some of your famous tea for a nightcap, or for once would you care for something stronger? I've got a bottle of champagne in my room—shall I bring it down to the bar and ask for some ice?'

Olivia looked at him for a moment, then threw caution to the winds. 'Why not get the ice sent up and bring the champagne to my room?'

His eyes narrowed. 'Your room?'

'Yes.' She shrugged. 'We sat in yours the other night. And mine here is twice the size of those at the Nerone. It's early yet, and I don't fancy sitting in the bar down here——'

'Would that have something to do with your encounter in the garden earlier? The bloody man's staring at you right this minute from a table by the window,' said Max hotly.

'Just get the ice,' said Olivia hastily.

She ran up two flights of stairs, and arrived in her room breathless with suppressed excitement. She stared at herself in the great mirror over the side-board, smiling defiantly at the reflection of a woman whose eyes glittered with something Olivia recognised belatedly as happiness. The smile faltered for a moment, then she shrugged. The die was cast. If Max read more into her suggestion than she intended, so be it. Her reflection smiled back confidently. Even on such short acquaintance she was certain Max would take her invitation in the spirit it was given, despite his self-confessed lack of charm and finesse.

Olivia turned away, her smile fading. She'd encountered charm and tact and finesse before in the person of Anthony, and none of it had been anything more than skin deep. With Anthony the charm had been a mask for his true personality, whereas with Max Hamilton she was ready to swear that what you saw was what you got.

When the expected knock came on the door Olivia flung it open and laughed at the sight of Max with a bottle of champagne under his arm, a silver bucket of ice in one hand and two champagne flutes in the other.

'I just got a very suspicious look from a dowager strung with pearls,' he said, grinning. 'She obviously thought I was up to no good at all.'

Olivia giggled as she took the glasses from him. 'You should have invited her to join us.'

'And rounded up your distinguished admirer to make a fourth!' Max whistled as he took in the room. 'I see what you mean—are you sure they knew you were travelling alone?'

'Oh, yes. I'm required to report on high-standard accommodation, remember—one of the perks of the job.' Olivia kicked off her shoes and curled up on the sofa, smiling at him. 'This is the second time you've plied me with champagne. Is it a habit of yours?'

Max left the bottle to chill and sat down beside her. 'Actually I was taking this one home to open at a suitable point before Drew left for the church, but this is a much better idea. Not,' he added, 'that you'll drink much of it, I know, but when you do drink anything it's usually white wine of some kind, so what better way to round off our final evening in Italy?'

'None,' she assured him. She eyed him warily. 'Were you surprised when I suggested my room for the purpose?'

'Very—not to mention delighted.' Max smiled. 'And I promise I won't read anything into it other than a far more satisfactory way to round off the evening than downstairs in the bar. Particularly,' he added, eyes narrowed, 'under the eyes of your Lothario of the garden.'

'How you do go on about him!'

'If you'd been here on your own he'd have moved in on you like a shot.'

'No, he wouldn't.'

'Why not?'

'I speak from experience,' she said serenely. 'I do this kind of thing a lot, remember. I often get overtures from men in hotels. I'm used to dispensing with unwanted company.'

'So why was it different with me?' he asked swiftly.

'In the beginning it was no different at all. If you cast your mind back, Max Hamilton, you may remember I was pretty incensed by your initial overtures. If I hadn't been worried about Sophie I wouldn't have given you the time of day.'

Max sighed heavily. 'And there was I, convinced it was a case of love at first sight!'

'No, you weren't,' she retorted, laughing. 'At our first meeting all you saw was a stranger you were sure held the key to the mystery of the vanishing brother. I doubt you even noticed I was a woman!'

Max snorted in derision. 'I may lack subtlety, but I do possess twenty-twenty vision, Olivia! I noticed you were a woman all right. Though I admit you gave me the shock of my life when you took your sunglasses off,' he said gruffly. 'Up to that point I'd looked on you as just a cold, hostile female hell bent on obstructing my efforts to find out about Drew. Then——'

'Then I took off my glasses and you said, "My God, Miss Smith, you're beautiful", just like they did in all those black and white films,' she teased.

He shook his head, grinning. 'Not quite. I wasn't so blind that I couldn't see you were a good-looking woman——'

'Gee, thanks!'

'Stop interrupting! What I'm trying to explain—very badly, obviously—is that when you took off those enormous black lenses and I saw your eyes and face leap out at me in glorious Technicolor, I was stunned.'

'Were you?' she asked, suddenly very serious.

He nodded. 'And you smiled. For the first time that evening, as I remember it. I looked into those fabulous green eyes and saw that mouth curve in a smile which gave me such a sudden, violent urge to kiss you I made a run for it before I ruined any hope of further contact between us.'

Olivia gazed at him, fascinated. 'I had no idea!'

'That was obvious,' he said drily, and got up to open the champagne. 'This should be chilled enough by now.' He removed the cork efficiently, filled two glasses and handed her one as he sat down close to her again.

'To our respective siblings and their future happiness,' said Olivia, raising her glass.

'I second that,' said Max, drank, then raised his glass again. 'But now for a special toast of my own. To a pair of beautiful eyes the sea-green colour of Venus.'

'The colour of Venus?' she repeated, intrigued.

Max nodded. 'Didn't you know that the colour green has a certain mysticism——?'

'Oh, no, not you as well,' she said with distaste, and Max took her hand.

'Listen, Olivia,' he said forcefully. 'Forget your husband's fixation about green and bad luck. In most cultures green is the colour of hope. The Greeks called it the colour of Venus, because she was born from the depths of the sea, and legend has it that at moments of passion her eyes glowed with green fire. Do yours?' he added abruptly.

Colour rose in her cheeks again. 'I wouldn't know,' she said shortly, and turned her head away, but Max caught her chin in his hand and turned her face up to his. He looked down into her eyes for a long, tense moment, then he kissed them shut, and moved his lips slowly down over her face until they found her mouth.

A violent tremor ran through Olivia at his touch, and Max raised his head and took her glass from her lax fingers, then drew her into his arms and kissed her again, his caressing hands moulding her close against him, his mouth wooing hers with a slow, mounting demand which roused an almost unbearable excitement which shook her to her depths. Eyes closed, she melted against him, the fingers of one hand thrust through the hair which curled over his collar. She surrendered herself to the sheer joy of the moment, responding ardently to the hard, expert mouth which coaxed hers apart with such subtlety a shock of reaction ran through her at the sudden, sensuous demand of his tongue. She gasped at the white-hot dart of fire through her breasts as his fingers caressed her nipples through the thin silk of her dress, and she stiffened, arching away involuntarily. Max's embrace loosened and he looked down into her eyes in question.

'Not so very large a transgression,' he said very quietly.

She buried her face suddenly against his shoulder. 'I know,' she said, muffled. 'I'm a fool. There's an ugly word for women who tease. Not that I meant to. But you could be forgiven for reading more into an invitation to my room than I meant. My defence would never hold up in court, would it!'

Max held her close, smoothing her hair with a long hand. 'Olivia, I know perfectly well you weren't inviting me to bed. But hell—I'm not a eunuch. You're very beautiful, and we've just spent an evening together that can only be described as romantic, over-worked hackneyed word though it is. I could no more help kissing you and touching you than breathing. Do you want me to go?'

'No!' she said vehemently, and drew away to look up into his frowning, watchful face. 'That's just it. I very much want you to stay. I like being with you, and I wanted you to kiss me.' She drew in a deep, unsteady breath. 'But I have a long-standing problem with that. It happens whenever a man comes near me, unfortunately, and I don't mean I'm attracted to my own sex, either, in case you're wondering.'

'I'm not,' he assured her, frowning. 'So what's the problem, Olivia?'

'I've been told I'm frigid,' she said flatly. 'You don't know it, but I'm actually paying you a compliment by even admitting it. Normally I keep the sad fact to myself. Bitter experience taught me that most men look on it as a challenge.'

He nodded slowly, his eyes oddly tender. 'Sure they can be the one to cure you!'

Olivia managed a wry, shaky smile. 'Exactly. Which is why my life is fairly empty of male company, other than one or two who are friends in the truest sense. Even if I meet someone I like enough to go out with I don't, because I just can't face the inevitable hassle.'

Max frowned. 'Yet for a while you seemed to respond, to be perfectly happy in my arms. It was only when I tried to take a step further—a very ordinary, routine sort of step, incidentally—that you stiffened like a ramrod and tried to pull away.'

Olivia thrust a hand through her hair dejectedly. 'I didn't mean to. I didn't even want to. Stupid, isn't it? I'm thirty years old, not thirteen!'

With care Max drew her against him, her head on his shoulder as he held her in a light, protective embrace she surrendered to with a little sigh of despair.

'So it isn't repugnance for my person that's the problem,' he commented thoughtfully, 'otherwise you'd be up and away right now.'

'No,' said Olivia, and burrowed closer to show she meant it. 'I like being close to you like this. I feel safe.'

'Thanks!' he said drily. 'That's a first, anyway. To my knowledge no woman's described me as safe before.'

She raised her head to smile at him. 'Sorry. I must be very bad for your ego.'

'That can take care of itself,' he assured her. 'I'm more concerned with yours. It should be in very good working order, lord knows, with one man—myself— very much at your service, and Mr Valentino downstairs all too obviously wishing he were in my shoes.'

'I bet he wouldn't be right now!' said Olivia, regaining her sense of humour. 'Not, of course, that I'd have invited *him* to my room.'

'Wise move. With him you really wouldn't have been safe, believe me!'

'I know. But I knew you meant it when you said you wouldn't rush me into bed.' Olivia turned her eyes up to his. 'To be honest I truly believed that if you did I wouldn't object. I *hoped* I wouldn't object. You're the first man I've felt attracted to physically since—since Anthony died.'

Max stared. 'So when you asked me up here you honestly considered the possibility that we'd make love?'

She nodded, depressed. 'So if it didn't happen for you, it's never going to happen with anyone.'

'And that matters to you?'

Her eyes flashed green fire. 'Of course it does! I don't fancy marriage again, but I want to feel I'm normal, with all a normal woman's urges, even have some kind of lasting relationship.' She halted, eyeing him ruefully. 'Don't be nervous. Even if you had performed the sexual miracle I wouldn't have demanded instant commitment! But at least I'd have had hope. And now I don't, green eyes or not. There's something radically wrong with me I can't put right. Max, I've never told anyone this before. I *said* you should have been a priest. All I do is confess painful, private secrets to you.'

'I sure as hell don't feel like a priest,' he said grimly, and pulled her back into his arms. 'Come here, Olivia. For God's sake have a good cry and get it all out of your system.'

She shook her head emphatically, but something in his voice touched a chord deep inside her, opening the floodgate on tears which overwhelmed her at first, to the point where she could hardly breathe. Max held her tightly until the storm abated a little then mopped her up efficiently with his handkerchief, and held her close, smoothing back her dishevelled hair when she lay spent at last against his shoulder.

'There,' he said gruffly at last. 'Do you feel better?'

'No,' she said thickly. 'Sorry to be ungrateful, but I feel a damn sight worse.'

He raised her face to his and chuckled. 'You look a lot worse, too!'

'Thanks!'

'Don't mention it. All part of the Hamilton service. Have some more champagne.'

The chilled wine felt like nectar to Olivia's tear-hoarse throat, but after only a mouthful or two she put the glass down.

'Any more of that and I won't have a secret I can call my own,' she said huskily, and managed a commendably cheerful smile. 'I bet the dowager you met would be surprised if she could see us now.'

Max tightened his arm about her. 'She's probably sitting bolt upright in bed, quivering with curiosity about the orgy she imagines we're enjoying.'

Olivia smiled ruefully. 'Instead of which you've been forced into the cork-shouldered Father Confessor role again. Sorry, Max.'

'I'm not,' he assured her, so matter-of-factly that she had no doubt he was telling the truth. 'I only wish I could do something to help.' He hesitated. 'Was this the reason your marriage broke down, Olivia?' A shudder ran through her and he held her tightly. 'Sorry—didn't mean to trespass.'

She shook her head vehemently. 'You may as well know it all. As it happens my little problem is the effect, not the cause of the break-up.'

'So you had no objection to your husband's love-making,' said Max in a rather odd tone.

'No. Quite the reverse.' Olivia leaned against him wearily, her head against his shoulder as she stared unseeingly across the room.

'Will it help to tell me what happened?' he asked carefully.

'I don't know. I've never told anyone before.' She twisted round to look up at him. 'Are you sure you want to hear all this?'

'Hell, Olivia, surely you can tell I'm burning with curiosity!' he said bluntly. 'But if it's something you'd rather keep to yourself——'

'Up to now I've hardly been able to think about it, let alone talk,' she said quickly, settling back against his shoulder. 'But with you it's different.'

Olivia was silent for a moment, then, slowly, choosing her words with care, she began to tell him how Anthony Maitland had come into the travel agency where she worked to arrange a holiday for his mother. Anthony had been the only child of quite elderly parents, and his father died when his young son was eight.

'So he was brought up alone with his mother,' said Max.

'Not entirely. Her older unmarried sister went to live with them when Anthony's father died. Those two women utterly adored him, indulged him in every whim all his life.'

'Was he good-looking?' asked Max gruffly.

'Beautiful, rather. Thick chestnut hair, bright blue eyes and a smile that could charm birds from a tree.'

The smile conquered Olivia from the first. Love at first sight was the literal truth after her first meeting with Anthony Maitland, and, to her joy, he had returned the feeling in full force. Soon they were spending as much time together as humanly possible, both of them so feverishly responsive to each other it was agony to part each night. Anthony made love to her with a skill Olivia thrilled to, every nerve in her body clamouring for sexual fulfilment. But Anthony, like the perfect gentleman she knew him to be, was determined to wait until their wedding-night before making love to her, with the result that seven weeks from their first meeting, and much against the wishes of both her father and Anthony's mother, they were married at a register office in a hasty, swift ceremony hardly worthy of the name. After a wedding breakfast attended only by Henry Collins and Sophie, and Mrs Maitland and her sister Lydia, the newlyweds flew off to a castle in Spain for their honeymoon.

CHAPTER EIGHT

IT WAS meant to be the perfect honeymoon, the flawless start to a life of bliss. Instead, Olivia, told Max unemotionally, it was a nightmare.

'Right from the start?' he said quietly.

'Yes.' She shivered. 'It was a disaster. And not because I wasn't willing to enter into the spirit of the thing, believe me.'

Olivia had gone gladly into the arms of her wildly impatient husband, but after a prolonged session of kisses and caresses, far longer than she'd expected, or wanted, the new bride realised something was wrong. Very wrong. Despite her passionate response it eventually became obvious that Anthony was physically incapable of consummating their marriage.

'You mean he was a homosexual?' asked Max gently.

Olivia's eyes dropped. 'No. He wasn't. I think, in a way, I could have understood it better if he had been.'

'Then why?'

'Good question. The problem, he swore, only arose with me.'

Max turned her face up to his. 'Did you believe him?'

'Of course I did!' She smiled scathingly. 'What did *I* know!'

'You'd never had a lover before?'

'Not in the way you mean. I'd had boyfriends, but nothing serious.' She smiled wryly. 'I was filled with highflown notions about being a good example to Sophie, and sparing my father any worry—and, to be honest, I never met anyone I wanted that way until Anthony.'

'What did he do for a living?'

'He worked for a merchant bank—sort of stockbroker, I suppose. I thought it madly glamorous when I met him.' She smiled sardonically. 'I was the lowly little assistant in a travel agency, going to nightschool so I could get promotion. Anthony dazzled me.'

'So what happened when the honeymoon went wrong?' asked Max, frowning.

Olivia's eyes darkened. 'We spent three days—and nights—of misery in a fairy-tale castle near Cordoba. Anthony forced me to do the most degrading things to try and put matters right, telling me it must be my fault, that it had never happened before, that the weeks of frustration before our wedding must have done some kind of damage.'

'You believed that?' he said incredulously.

'I was in such a state I didn't know what to believe. After three days, Anthony decided we must go home, that back on familiar ground everything would be all right. He was wrong—if anything, it was worse.'

Far from effecting a cure, life in the new flat became so unbearable that Anthony took to coming home later and later from the bank, until one night he was out until dawn. He came home wild-eyed and elated, his eyes glittering with triumph, to tell Olivia that his problem was definitely her fault.

'He'd proved it by picking up a girl,' said Olivia tonelessly. 'Apparently with her the encounter had been a raging success, worth every penny he'd paid for it.'

'Did he leave you alone after that?'

'No.' She shuddered and Max pulled her closer. 'He was convinced he was cured, and this was only months after we were married, remember. He swore he was still in love with me.'

'How did you feel about him?'

'I still cared for him. But when the visit to the prostitute triggered off a new onslaught to mend matters between us life was hell. Nothing had changed—he was still impotent with me. The beautiful young man I'd been so in love with lost his veneer of charm entirely, and turned into a raging, hysterical maniac.'

'Why didn't you leave him?' demanded Max in disgust. 'You'd have had ample grounds for annulment.'

'I thought of it, believe me! But eventually Anthony gave up trying with me, which made life easier to bear. Then——' She stopped, swallowing.

'What happened next?' he prompted gently.

'By this time we'd stopped sharing a bed and a life,' Olivia went on doggedly. 'I worked all the overtime I could, studied hard, and Anthony spent more and more time away from the flat, alternating between his doting mother and aunt and, as he was always ready to tell me, the pleasure of bought sex. Not surprisingly his work suffered and the inevitable happened. He got the sack shortly after I got promotion. He couldn't bear it. He cried and raged like a demented child, then flung out of the flat to drive to his mother's for consolation. On the way an articulated lorry jacknifed across a dual carriageway and he ploughed into it. The police told me he must have died instantly.'

'Hell, what a mess,' said Max gruffly, and pulled her on to his lap, to hold her against his shoulder like a child. 'When was this?'

'Four years ago,' she said wearily, rubbing her cheek against him. 'I sold the flat in Cheltenham and transferred to the London branch of the firm when he died.' She looked up at him. 'Sophie doesn't know anything about this, by the way. I couldn't even tell my father, because he was dead against Anthony from the start.'

'With good reason. The bastard has a lot to answer for,' said Max savagely, and suddenly, without warning, he bent his head and kissed her hard, his arms tightening around her. 'Don't worry,' he said unevenly, raising his head. 'You've nothing to fear from me, I swear.'

'I know,' she said breathlessly. 'I just wish——'

'So do I,' he said, and smiled into her tear-smudged eyes. 'But instead of just wishing I intend to do something constructive about it.'

'What, exactly?'

'To start with, once we're back in England I intend to see as much of you as I possibly can.'

'Why?' she asked baldly.

'Because I think we could be very good friends, Olivia.' His eyes held hers. 'I think that in time we could be lovers, too. But if that never happens I'm damned if it's any impediment to seeing each other on a regular basis.'

'You really mean that?' she said, moved.

'Yes.' He smiled, stroking her cheek with his hand. 'I'm thirty-eight, Olivia, not a randy teenager.'

'A week ago I didn't even know you,' said Olivia obliquely.

He smiled. 'Time's relative. Soon you'll wonder how you existed before you met me.'

'You're very sure of yourself!'

'I'm sure of you, too, Olivia.'

'Are you, now?' she retorted, struggling upright.

'Sure that one day you'll enjoy a perfectly normal, passionate relationship with a man.'

'Will your crystal ball tell you the name of the lucky prizewinner?' she asked drily.

'I know that already,' he assured her, so supremely confident that Olivia's heart missed a beat. 'But now it's time I went.' He put her gently on her feet and got up, turning her face up to his. 'If I run into my dowager again I'll do my best to look suitably ravished not to disappoint her.'

She giggled, and he nodded in approval.

'That's better. No more tears, Olivia.'

'I rarely allow myself any,' she said tartly. 'And never in company!'

'Then I count myself privileged.' He bent his head and kissed her, taking his time over it, but with no other attempt to touch her. 'You see?' he said, raising his head. 'A kiss between friends.'

'This isn't the way I meant the evening to end,' she said wistfully.

Something leapt in his eyes for an instant and his arms reached for her involuntarily, then with a smile he dropped them and kissed the tip of her nose instead. 'What time did you order breakfast sent up in the morning?'

'Seven.'

'Right. I'll meet you in the foyer at seven-thirty.'

*   *   *

The journey back to London was uneventful, with a smooth flight and a punctual arrival on a day grey with rain.

'Home, sweet home,' said Max, grinning, as they waited for their luggage.

Olivia pulled a face. 'I hope the weather's better than this for the wedding.'

'It's got time to improve before then.' He loaded their bags on a trolley and hurried with her towards the exit.

In the taxi on the way back Max held her hand in his, his promise of the night before implicit in the hard warm grasp.

'How soon can I see you?' he demanded as they drew up outside a large Edwardian house in a quiet leafy street in Ealing.

'When are you going down to join Drew?'

'A day or so before the wedding.' Max handed her out then followed her with her luggage. 'I've got some work to catch up on before then—I wasn't intending to go junketing off to Italy on my way home.'

'Then you won't have any more time for "junketing" right now then,' she teased, and he grinned and tapped an admonishing finger on her cheek.

'Not so pert, young Olivia. I'll leave you in peace tonight, but how about tomorrow?'

'Fine.'

'I'll take you out for a meal——'

'After all that hotel food, wouldn't you like to sample my cooking?' She waved a hand at the top floor of the red-brick house. 'I live up there. Ring my bell about eightish—and now you'd better get in the taxi or the fare will be ruinous!'

Max kissed her quickly, then sprinted through the rain to the waiting cab. 'Eight,' he called, and waved a hand as he got in.

Olivia rang her father, had a chat with him to report on Sophie and her Andrea, told him she'd be home ten days later for the weekend to go to a wedding, then rang the Bellagio and had a word with Sophie, who was obviously very much on duty and not able to say much.

'I'll ring you later with a phone-card,' promised her sister. '*Ciao!*'

There was just enough time for a swift visit to the shops to stock her fridge and kitchen cupboards, then Olivia had a bath and went through her mail before heating a bowl of soup and making herself a toasted sandwich.

When the phone rang later that evening she was surprised, but inordinately pleased to hear Max's deep, already familiar tones instead of Sophie, as expected.

'How are you settling in?' he asked.

'As well as can be expected,' said Olivia ruefully, eyeing the rain streaming down her windows.

'Does that mean you've got any left-over blues from last night?'

'No!' she answered promptly, very pleased to find this was the truth. 'I meant the rain. It's such steady, relentless stuff—nothing like the passion and drama of that downpour in Asolo!'

'After three months without any rain at all I like it.'

'I keep forgetting your sojourn among the camels.'

'I've got a pile of paperwork in front of me as a reminder,' he said gloomily. 'If I'm a little late tomorrow night, bear with me. It's usually hectic when I get back to base after one of these trips.'

'We could leave it until the following night if you like,' she offered.

'Not on your life!' he said promptly. 'Just don't go to too much trouble over the meal.'

'I won't. I'm working tomorrow too.'

'What an industrious pair we are!' he mocked. 'But seriously, don't make anything that's likely to spoil. An engineer's social life can be as uncertain as a doctor's.' He paused. 'Perhaps I should warn you that this has put paid to more than one relationship in the past.'

'I'll probably just open a tin!' she said cheerfully. 'So don't expect too much.'

'I shall hope, rather than expect! Goodnight, Olivia.'

When the phone rang again a moment or two later Olivia was unsurprised to hear Sophie, sounding indignant.

'Who were you talking to, Liv? You were engaged for ages.'

'Max Hamilton,' said Olivia baldly, opting for the truth. 'He's coming round tomorrow evening for a meal.' When she went on to explain that Max had also accompanied her to Asolo, Sophie was astonished.

'My word, he's a quick worker, Liv! And you must really like him, because usually you're such a slow coach with men. Not that I blame you,' she added hastily. 'I mean I know you took ages to get over Anthony, and he wasn't exactly the ideal husband and all that——'

'How do you know that?' demanded Olivia, startled.

'I wasn't blind, Liv! I mean, anyone could see things weren't exactly bliss. So be careful with Max Hamilton, please.'

'Yes, Grandma. Why so worried?'

'He's a bit different from Anthony.'

'Probably that's what attracts me.'

'Oh, well, he must be reasonably all right, because Andrea likes him.'

'That's all that matters, then!'

'You may well laugh, but I feel sort of responsible.'

'Sophie, darling, I'm a big girl. I have other men friends, remember.'

'Not like Max Hamilton!'

This was true enough, Olivia conceded, after Sophie rang off. Max was something quite outside her previous experience of men. Odd, really, after knowing him such a short time, that she was so certain of his integrity.

She told him so the following evening.

'That's good to hear,' he said gravely. 'After the way we met, I hardly hoped for such a vote of confidence at this stage.'

'What stage is that?' she queried.

'The delicate minefield of getting to know each other gradually.' His eyes locked with hers. 'It's hard for me to proceed with care.'

'Why?'

'Because I feel I know you so well. Maybe we met in another life. There must be some explanation for this gut-feeling of familiarity with you.'

'You make me sound like an old shoe,' she teased, helping him to pasta. 'Have some salad. I dressed it with basil and olive oil to remind us of Italy.'

'I'll never need reminders,' he said with such emphasis they were still for a moment, looking at each other across her small table. 'Not of the past few days there with you, at least,' he added.

'That's a very nice thing to say,' she said huskily, and turned her attention to her plate. 'How was your day? You weren't late after all.'

'I told everyone I had something much better to do with my time than spend it mulling over feasibility reports,' he said, grinning. 'Quite surprised a couple of my colleagues. I'm a famed workaholic.'

'So am I,' she admitted, smiling. 'Perhaps it's time for both of us to slow down and enjoy the lighter side of life more.'

'Amen to that—let's do it together!'

When it was time for Max to go Olivia was surprised by her reluctance to part with him.

'What is it?'

'Nothing. It's early, that's all.'

'Would you like me to stay longer?'

'Yes.'

'Good. I was being polite—trying not to outstay my welcome!' Max returned to the sofa and pulled her down with him. 'Let's discuss arrangements for our trip to Gloucestershire.'

Olivia, secretly astonished with herself for importuning him to stay, looked at him warily. 'Have you told Drew I'm coming?'

He grinned. 'Damn right I have. He's burning with curiosity.'

'But you must have had other women in your life?'

'Of course. But this is the first time I've ever taken one to a family occasion like this. Drew's convinced I've met my Waterloo.'

'I only hope he won't be disappointed!'

Max put a finger under her chin and raised her face to his. 'He'll be dazzled, and every other man there under the age of eighty will envy me.'

She sighed and pulled away. 'It's only the outer wrapping they'll see. If they knew me better they wouldn't envy you at all.'

Max drew her back gently, taking her into his arms. He bent and kissed her, and she closed her eyes, shivering a little as his lips roved over her eyelids and nose and cheeks, before settling on her mouth. 'You see?' he said huskily, moving a fraction away. 'Perfectly painless—and I won't break my promise. If you and I ever progress beyond this stage, Olivia, it's up to you to make the move.'

'And if I never do?' she said unevenly.

'Then we'll go on as we are, just good friends.' He kissed her again, then got up. 'Now I really must go. You look tired.'

'Which means I look like a hag!' she said, smiling valiantly as she jumped to her feet.

'Anything less like a hag would be hard to imagine,' he said drily. 'Now,' he went on, suddenly businesslike, 'I'm tied up for the next couple of nights. Are you free on Saturday? Let's go out for the day.'

Olivia eyed him curiously. 'What do you usually do at weekends?'

'Work, more often than not. For you I'll make an exception!'

'Then I can hardly refuse,' she said demurely.

*   *   *

Sometimes, in the days that followed, Olivia could hardly remember what she'd done with her life before meeting Max Hamilton. Her colleagues teased her about a new sparkle in her eye and a definite spring in her step. And when one of her schoolfriends rang up to find she was booked solid for the next few days he whistled and teased her with well-worn gibes about merry widows.

Olivia ground her teeth, and because she'd known him since she was twelve told him she'd cross him off her list if he ever used the phrase again. He begged mercy and said he'd ring again when her itinerary was less hectic.

When she mentioned this to Max he told her, in no uncertain terms, that this was unlikely to occur.

'Any spare time you've got you spend with me,' he said flatly.

Olivia almost missed her footing as they went up the stairs to her flat. She shot him a startled look. 'Do you really mean that?'

'Of course I do,' he retorted, frowning at her. 'I always say what I mean.' He shrugged. 'I may go over the top a bit when I lose my temper, but otherwise I don't deal in cross-talk. Can't you believe that?'

She unlocked her door and he followed her inside. They'd had dinner in a Thai restaurant within walking distance from her flat, and the evening had been the usual quickfire exchange of conversation and opinions, none of it on a personal level until now.

She looked up at him in appeal, a wry little smile curving her mouth. 'I suppose I keep thinking——'

'That's the trouble with you,' he said roughly, taking her in his arms. 'Stop thinking for a while— let your feelings take over.'

He kissed her ruthlessly, stilling her first instinctive struggles with arms like iron bars, and went on kissing her with growing, hot demand. To her astonishment Olivia found herself responding, hesitantly at first, then as though the floodgates had opened she met his hunger in kind, overwhelmed by such a sudden rush of unfamiliar desire she shook from head to foot, and Max held her cruelly tight, fired by her hesitant response, all the restraint he'd exercised in the past few days suddenly gone. Their breathing mingled raggedly and he slid a seeking hand down her spine to cup her bottom hard against him. She gasped at the thrust of hard, male need against her, surrendering to the invasion of his demanding tongue, and for a long, mindless interval they stood locked in each other's arms, deaf and blind to anything other than the primeval forces joining them together in mutual need.

Then suddenly Max let her go and stood back, his face colourless under the deep-dyed tan. His eyes blazed with suppressed desire and Olivia stared back, dazed.

'I didn't mean to do that,' he said through his teeth, loosening his tie. 'I told myself I could stay cool, whatever happened, however much I wanted you. It seems I can't.'

Olivia drew in a deep, unsteady breath. 'You must have noticed something——'

'Are you joking?' he demanded, thrusting a hand through his hair. 'I was blind to anything but the feel of you in my arms . . .' His eyes lit with sudden heat. 'Unless——'

'The penny's dropped?' She gave him a rather wobbly smile. 'It was you who called the halt, Max, not me.'

With a triumphant smile he held out his arms. Olivia walked into them and rested her head against his chest and Max hugged her close.

'Is this a breakthrough, Olivia?'

She lifted her face to him and smiled. 'I rather think it must be. It's certainly never happened before—I mean, not since——'

He stopped her words with a kiss, then raised his head to smile down into her dazed green eyes. 'Such surprise is hardly flattering, darling.'

Her eyelids flickered at the endearment, and he grinned and pulled her down to sit beside him on the sofa.

'You still look surprised,' he commented drily. 'I suppose you thought that the least sign of encouragement on your part and I'd be dragging you off to bed by your hair, determined to have my wicked way immediately.'

Olivia giggled, immensely reassured. 'Well—yes. I wouldn't have blamed you. I told you I always panicked past a certain point. You could have taken it for a green light when the panicking never happened.'

'The only green light I'm interested in, darling, is the one in those beautiful eyes of yours.' His mouth twisted. 'Besides, like a fool I said any initiative would have to come from you. Which is why I slammed on the brakes, though how the hell I managed it I'll never know.' He looked down at her, his eyes holding hers. 'Why, Olivia? What was so different tonight?'

She felt colour rise in her face and hid against his shoulder. 'There's no polite way to put this,' she muttered, 'but after what happened—or didn't happen—with Anthony, I think it was the discovery that—well, that you were obviously——'

'Not afflicted in the same way,' he completed for her, and turned her face up to his. 'Is that what you've been afraid of all along with other men? That when it came to the point the same thing would happen?'

She shook her head vehemently. 'No! At least if it was I didn't realise it. There was never any thinking through about it, just blind instinct. Once any man tried to do more than kiss me I froze, and wanted to run.'

'So what's different with me?' he demanded.

She shrugged. 'Maybe you were more persistent,' she said casually, then gasped as he pulled her close and began kissing her in a way which soon made it very clear to them both that the first time had been no fluke. Olivia yielded to him in full measure to the point that a little later Max told her roughly that he must go now or he'd never go at all.

'You don't have to go,' she said unevenly.

'Yes, I do,' he returned, his face grim as he drew her to his feet. 'Tonight we've made progress, Olivia. But if I took you to bed you'd probably regret it in the morning. And when I do make love to you—as I'm going to one day—or one night—soon, I want it to be so good for you that the ghost of your first marriage will be laid for all time.'

First marriage? thought Olivia in alarm.

'That's right,' he said, reading her thoughts. 'Your second marriage will be to me. And don't tell me this is too soon, because only time can mend that particular problem. I mean to have you, Olivia—I've told you that before.'

She pushed back her hair, eyeing him warily. 'I didn't think you meant marriage!'

'I didn't think I did, either, in the beginning. It took me at least two days into knowing you to realise that!'

Olivia drew in a deep breath. 'I'm deeply flattered——'

'*Flattered*!' he retorted, scowling.

'Yes, flattered. Any woman would be. But I don't want to get married. Not even to you,' she added, her voice trailing away at the look in his eyes.

'So what was all that about just now?' he demanded furiously.

'That was about finding I'm normal and you're obviously a terrific lover and we could be happy together!'

He closed the space between them, towering over her menacingly, but she put out a hand and kept him at arm's length, her eyes brilliant with appeal.

'Try to understand, Max. I rushed into marriage before. Next time, if there *is* a next time, I'd want to live with you—or whoever—for a time first——'

'Take the goods on approval until you're sure they'll suit!'

'No,' she snapped, suddenly illogically angry. 'Just a sensible effort to make things work this time. Why are you so shocked, for heaven's sake? It's what most people do——'

'But you're not "most people", and neither am I,' he retorted. 'I'm thirty-eight years old and until I met you I was diametrically opposed to marriage. The thought of spending the rest of my life with one woman was anathema to me.' He gave a short, mirthless laugh. 'It's the biter bit, I suppose. The one woman I want to marry prefers to co-habit without a marriage certificate—quite a bodyblow to my ego.'

'I don't see why,' said Olivia hotly. 'The very fact that I'm ready to—to "cohabit" should boost your wretched ego. I couldn't even stand the thought of a lover—until I met you.'

'I'm not asking for a couple of one-night stands,' he said angrily. 'Or even a year or two of living together. I want you for life. And if you don't feel the same for me there's no point in going on with this.'

'Fine!' She marched to the door and flung it open. 'You were right. I'm very much obliged to you for your restraint. It would have been a mistake to stay together tonight—or any other night! Just—just go.'

Max slammed the door shut again and yanked her into his arms. 'Listen to me, Olivia,' he said through his teeth. 'I intend to be your lover, and I intend to marry you, but I warn you now if you ever again tell me to go in that tone of voice I will. And I won't be back.'

Dark eyes blazed down into furious green ones, and for a moment or two the entire, delicate structure of their burgeoning relationship tottered on the brink of destruction. The silence grew and filled the room like a living thing, then Olivia tore her eyes away and Max let her go.

'At the risk of sounding repetitious,' she said tonelessly, 'did you mean that?'

Max thrust a hand through his hair. 'To a certain extent I did,' he said, scrupulously truthful. 'It isn't every day a proposal of marriage gets thrown back in my face. I can be forgiven for losing my temper slightly.'

A shadow of a smile played at the corners of her mouth. 'Slightly!' She sniffed. 'But I haven't changed my mind.'

He shrugged. 'Neither have I.'

They eyed each other questioningly.

'So what now?' asked Olivia.

'We go on as before, but with an added zest to the relationship.' Max smiled confidently. 'It'll be interesting to see who gives way first.'

'It won't be me,' she retorted.

His smile deepened. 'Want to bet?'

'Anything you like!'

Max thought for a while. 'All right. If you win I'll give you a pair of emerald earrings. If I win——' He frowned.

'Well?' she demanded, foot tapping.

'I'll have to ponder on that one. I'll tell you next time I see you!'

CHAPTER NINE

BUT the next time he saw her Max made no mention
of the bet, or the quarrel, and behaved as though the
new, passionate turn to their relationship had never
happened. He asked about her day, discussed the latest
cricket scores, asked if she fancied a trip to the play
the critics were raving about, then reverted, as they
usually did sooner or later, to the wedding. The family,
he told her, were meeting for a dinner party the night
before, but nothing Max could say would persuade
Olivia to accompany him to it, or meet any of his
family before the wedding.

'It wouldn't be fair. This is no time to divert any
interest from the big event,' she said firmly. 'I'll meet
you at the church. You can make the necessary introductions in the receiving line, just like everyone
else.'

'It means I won't see you for two days,' he said
morosely, as they parted on the Wednesday evening.
'Tomorrow, for my sins, I promised to be at Drew's
stag night.'

'You don't fancy the idea?'

He snorted. 'Drew's friends are all media types. I
stand out like a sore thumb.'

'Only because you're taller than most of them.'

He grinned. 'And about a hundred years older.'

'Maturity's *very* attractive,' she assured him,
smiling.

'I'm glad you think so.' He touched a finger to her bottom lip. 'Apart from my other obvious advantages over them, every man-jack of them will be stricken with envy when they see you.'

She pulled a face. 'I still have doubts about coming, you know. I never go to weddings. The last one I went to was my own.'

'After Drew's the next one will be yours too—and mine.' He pulled her close and kissed her until she melted against him, the new-found storm of response as much a shock and delight to her as the night before.

'I'll get my own way, you know,' he muttered between kisses. Indignant, she tried to push him away, but Max held her fast and in the end she surrendered to the giddy pleasure of mutual desire, even when it left them both shaken and wanting so much more.

'Very character-building,' he informed her raggedly. 'I'm not used to possessing my soul—and body—in such remarkable patience.'

'You don't have to,' she said challengingly, her eyes feverishly bright.

'Oh, yes, I do—at least until the day your defences crumble and you promise to marry me.' He shook her slightly, his eyes suddenly alight with amusement. 'This is bloody ridiculous, in some ways. We sound as though we're speaking each other's lines. It's usually the woman who holds out for a wedding-ring, not the other way round. Now kiss me and tell me you'll miss me until Saturday.'

This was easy to do, because it was the simple truth. What was less easy, Olivia found, once Max had gone, was ridding herself of a persistent, niggling thought that Anthony had insisted on a waiting game too. And the result of that was something she still couldn't bear to remember.

Knowing she was likely to excite a lot of unwanted interest at Drew Hamilton's wedding, Olivia had thought long and hard about what to wear. Reluctant to draw attention to herself, yet woman enough to want to look her best, she also had no intention of spending a great deal of money on the kind of outfit she'd have no use for afterwards. The early August weather was hot, and the outlook for the weekend good, so in her lunch hour next day Olivia bought a dramatic wide-brimmed hat in jade-green straw to wear with the ivory linen suit she'd worn the first time she met Max.

Her father was deeply pleased to see her when she arrived late on the Friday evening, and much reassured when she gave him her opinion of young Andrea Bartoli, and confirmed Sophie's well-being.

'And how about you, darling?' he asked later, when they were drinking coffee in the garden to enjoy the sunset. 'What wedding is this? Anyone I know?'

When Olivia filled him in a little on the details he eyed her closely, rather taken aback when he heard it was the young man from the television motoring programme he enjoyed.

'I met his brother Max in Italy,' said Olivia, her face warm. 'We get on rather well, actually. He's a consultant engineer.'

'You must have got on remarkably well for him to ask you to his brother's wedding,' chuckled her father. 'Will I get to meet this Max some time?'

'Possibly,' she said, smiling. 'But not yet awhile.'

'Still nervous of getting your fingers burnt a second time, Liv?'

'Something like that.' She gave him a wry smile. 'And maybe you won't like Max any better than Anthony.'

'I could hardly like him less, my child. And if this Max of yours is responsible for bringing the sparkle back to your eyes I'm predisposed to like him anyway!' His eyes twinkled. 'There's the telephone. Could this possibly by your new friend anxious to confirm your arrival in Gloucestershire?'

He was right. When she answered the phone, Max sounded irate when he demanded why the hell she hadn't rung him as soon as she'd arrived.

'I didn't think of it,' she said honestly. 'I'm seeing you in the morning anyway. How are you? A bit hungover from last night, by the sound of it.'

'I'm better now,' he said elliptically. 'I won't sully your ears with a description of my condition early this morning. Thank God Drew had the sense to arrange the affair for last night, not tonight. Otherwise there'd be a lot of very pallid, moaning male wedding-guests. I admit I had no enthusiasm for the celebratory dinner!'

'Serves you right,' said Olivia without sympathy. 'I thought you'd have had more sense.'

'I had a lot more sense than everyone else,' he retorted, 'the bridegroom included.'

'Just make sure he gets to the church in one piece tomorrow!'

'Not my job. That's the best man's prerogative. You're the one I'm concerned with tomorrow, Olivia Maitland.' His voice dropped a tone. 'Not having second thoughts about turning up, I trust!'

'It's the bride who gets nervous, not the guests,' she retorted. 'I said I'll come so I'll be there.'

With a twenty-mile drive in front of her Olivia began getting ready early next morning, to give herself plenty of time to arrive in the village of Horsleigh well before the appointed hour of noon. She hadn't been to Horsleigh for years, and her father informed her that a new road would take her there much quicker than the old country route she vaguely remembered. She took down some directions, then went to dress, finally presenting herself for inspection before she left.

Henry Collins eyed his daughter with loving admiration. 'Funny thing, Liv, when I don't see you for a while I forget how lovely you are. Splendid hat, darling. You'll be the smartest one there.'

Olivia smiled gratefully at her father. 'You're biased,' she told him, kissing him, but he shook his head.

'You've matured into a very beautiful woman, Olivia. I hope this Hamilton chap takes good care of you.'

'What harm can I come to at a wedding?' she parried lightly.

'I didn't mean that,' he said testily, and she smiled at him in reassurance.

'I know, Dad. But don't worry. This man's different.'

Because Max wanted to drive her back to London Olivia had travelled down by train. She set off for Horsleigh in her father's old saloon, conscious of an odd butterfly or two in her middle regions, but otherwise glad to find herself looking forward to the day. The sun was shining, the sky was blue, and shortly she would be with Max again.

She'd travelled about ten miles when the car began making worrying noises. Olivia pulled into the side of the road to investigate just as the car ground to a halt. She took off her hat and jacket, released the catch of the bonnet, and eyed the broken fan belt with malevolence. What a time to choose, she told it furiously, and slammed the bonnet down. She ground her teeth impotently, wondering how far she was from the nearest telephone. Cars were streaming by, but none of the drivers seemed to see her, of if they did, took no notice. Olivia looked at her watch and groaned. Only half an hour to go to the wedding and she was stranded ten miles or more from Horsleigh! At long last a Range Rover pulled in behind her and a young woman in jodhpurs jumped out, looking concerned.

'Can I help?'

Olivia's eyes lit up. 'My fan belt's gone, and I'm on my way to a wedding. Could you possibly ring the first garage you come to and ask them to come to my rescue?'

'I can do better than that,' said the girl blithely. 'I've got a mobile phone in the car. There's a garage about two miles further on. They know me. I'll get them on to it right away.'

Blessing her Good Samaritan, Olivia watched as the girl leapt into the car, saw her talking on the phone, then the girl's thumb went up in a victory gesture. As the Range Rover cruised past the kind young driver yelled 'Twenty minutes!' waved her hand and drove off.

It was more like half an hour by the time help was at hand, and seemed twice as long to Olivia as she

waited in the car, fuming, picturing Max's reaction
when she failed to turn up. A mechanic arrived in a
pick-up in due course, confirmed her diagnosis of
broken fan belt, and replaced it at commendable speed
when she told him about the wedding. Olivia paid him
then covered the ten miles to Horsleigh at a fraction
under the speed limit all the way, until the spire of
the church came into view. She parked at the end of
a long line of vehicles, sat still for a moment to
compose herself, then made some repairs to her face,
put on her jacket and settled the hat at the most be-
coming angle. She pulled on green suede gloves,
picked up her bag and got out of the car to walk towards the knot of onlookers at the lych-gate, cursing
the fates for making her late. As a child she'd always
had a horror of being late for church or school, and
something of the same feeling made her pulse beat
faster as she heard a choir singing 'Jesu, Joy of Man's
Desiring', and realised the wedding party must be in
the vestry, signing the register.

Deciding it was too late to go inside the church,
Olivia stayed where she was, and shortly afterwards
the strains of the triumphal 'Wedding March' organ
heralded the appearance of the bride and groom
through the church door.

Sarah and Drew Hamilton stood arm in arm, the
groom grinning from ear to ear, his blond hair
flopping across his forehead, his bride, serene and a
little pale in floating layers of organza, but with a
light in her eyes which brought a lump to Olivia's
throat. This, she thought, sighing, was exactly how a
wedding should be. Then a bevy of bridesmaids in
pink silk grouped round the happy pair, followed by
the rest of the family wedding party. Over the heads

of the others she saw Max's eyes pick her out, light
up, then narrow in angry question. She shrugged
apologetically, then stiffened as she saw the woman
clinging possessively to his arm as the photographer
and his assistant dodged about arranging everyone for
the official photographs. Max's companion was
blonde, and tremendously stylish in a slate-blue silk
suit cut to emphasise every curve, a small, frivolous
hat with a froth of veiling tilted low over eyes which
even from this distance Olivia saw were the same blue
as the dress.

The photographer asked the bride to kiss the groom
to immortalise the moment on film, which was the
signal for an exchange of kissing all round as the
blonde with Max reached up to pull his head down
to hers and plant a very lingering kiss on his mouth,
to a chorus of cat-calls from the groom and various
male guests.

Olivia watched on the fringe of the crowd, feeling
like a child outside the sweetshop window. She saw
Max's eyes searching for her and shrank back into
the shade of a yew tree, but a moment later he was
thrusting his way through the chattering guests to
confront her.

'What the hell happened?' he demanded without
ceremony.

'My fan belt broke on the way here,' she said,
equally baldly. 'I've only just arrived. Not,' she added
sweetly, 'that you seem to have missed me, or been
neglected in my absence.'

He looked at her in angry silence for a moment. 'I
was worried!'

'I couldn't help it,' she snapped, burning to know
who the blonde was, but ready to die rather than ask.

Max's name suddenly sounded on all sides.

'Another bloody photograph,' he said savagely, and gave her a steely look. 'Don't go away. I'll get this over with then come back for you and we can get out of here.'

'Surely you'll be missed at the reception?' she said, startled.

'Of course,' he said impatiently. 'I meant I can find a roundabout route to Sarah's home so we can have a moment to ourselves before I subject you to all the introductions——'

'*Max*!' roared his brother. 'We're waiting—come on.'

With a stifled curse Max eyed Olivia for a moment then turned on his heel and went to join his family for the group photograph. Olivia saw the blonde thrust her arm through Max's, smiling up at him in a proprietorial way as she stretched on tiptoe to whisper in his ear.

Heaven help me, I'm jealous! thought Olivia incredulously, and moved as inconspicuously as possible towards the lych-gate. She slipped through it, smiling brightly at the group of spectators waiting outside, and walked slowly towards her father's car, bitterly sorry she'd agreed to come. Before she reached the car she heard footsteps racing behind her and turned to face Max, who reached her precipitately, his face like thunder as he grasped her by the wrist.

'Running away?' he demanded.

'No. I just thought I'd stay out of the way until you had time for me.'

'*Time* for you? I got away as quickly as I can. It *is* my brother's wedding, remember!'

'Oh, I do. But I should never have agreed to come. I told you a wedding is no place for outsiders.'

'I don't know half the people here,' he said impatiently. 'And if you'd been on time you'd have been with me from the start, with none of this nonsense about outsiders.' He pulled her by the hand towards his car. 'Come on. Let's get out of here. We won't be missed for half an hour. Everyone will be too busy kissing everyone else back at the house to count heads.'

'There's been quite a lot of kissing already,' she said tightly. 'I saw you in fond embrace with the glamorous blonde.'

'Glamorous blonde?' he said blankly, opening the door for her, then he smiled mockingly. 'Are you jealous?' he asked silkily as he drove off.

'Of course not!' Olivia's chin lifted. 'If you cast your mind back I told you jealousy was something I'd never experienced.'

'So you did.' He cast a look at her profile. 'I remember everything you've said to me, as it happens.'

'Not too difficult,' she responded stiffly. 'We haven't known each other long.'

'Long enough.' He put a hand out to touch hers. 'You look very beautiful today, Olivia.'

'It's a miracle I'm not covered in oil stains,' she said lightly.

He questioned her about the incident, frowning at her acid tone when she informed him the only car which stopped to offer her help was driven by a woman.

'So you're off the entire male race today,' he commented in amusement.

'Oh, no. I'm very grateful to the mechanic who changed the fan belt—even if he was a bit condescending when he confirmed I was right about the fault.'

After another mile or so Max turned the car into a narrow lane which led along the edge of a wood, and stopped at a five barred gate.

'Now,' he said, turning to her. 'What's wrong?'

Olivia looked at him, thinking how impressive he looked in the formal black and grey of morning dress. 'Nothing's wrong, apart from the frustration of breaking down like that. I hate being late for anything. I'm sorry I wasn't there to see Sarah and Drew married.'

'The only wedding I want you punctual for is ours,' he said with emphasis, then narrowed his eyes at her withdrawn look. 'But I don't intend to get into an argument on that at this point. I'm powerless to do anything about it in the circumstances.'

'Or any circumstances!' Her eyes flashed, brilliantly green in the shadow of her hat.

His hand shot out to imprison hers. 'Fighting talk, Olivia. As I said before, I intend to have you, so you might as well get used to the idea first as last.'

Angered by his utter certainty, Olivia snatched her hand away. 'By which I take it that to enjoy the delights of your bed you're still adamant I have to marry you. Which in this day and age is utterly ludicrous. I object to ultimatums, so nothing doing.'

Max stared at her in silence, his face a hard, expressionless mask, and Olivia felt her anger drain away, and would have sold her soul to take the words back. They hung in the air between them, and try as she might to say she hadn't meant them, she found she couldn't utter the necessary words.

'If,' he said at last, turning back to the wheel, 'you'd be good enough to put in an appearance at the reception for a while I'd be grateful. I gave you quite an advance press. On a day like today, which should be the happiest one of Sarah's life, I don't want to trump up some flimsy excuse for your absence if you take off right now.'

Olivia swallowed. 'Of course. I've no wish to offend anyone.'

'You could have fooled me!' he said bitterly, and started the car, leaning towards her as he looked out of the back window to reverse into the lane. Aware of every line and pore in his skin, of the scent of him and his warmth, Olivia shrank away and his jaw tightened.

'Just stick it for half an hour,' he said coldly, 'then you can be away.'

Sarah's parents lived in an old converted farmhouse, surrounded by two acres of garden which made a beautiful setting for the reception in the August sunshine. Tables had been set out for the wedding breakfast under an awning on the terrace, there were flowers everywhere, in the borders, in flowerbeds and in tubs along the terrace and every table. Laughter and voices came out to greet them as Max handed Olivia out of the car in the paddock alongside the garden.

'The ground's dry,' he said briefly, glancing at her fragile shoes. 'You should be all right.'

'Of course,' she said quietly, and walked with him to the crowd of people gathered round the bride and groom in the centre of the lawn.

'Max,' shouted Drew Hamilton. 'Where the devil did you get to?'

'I brought Olivia the pretty way to give you time to get here first,' said Max, with a smile which stopped short of his eyes. 'Sarah, Drew, may I introduce Mrs Olivia Maitland.'

Her status, stressed very slightly, didn't go unnoticed, Olivia saw, smiling serenely.

'How do you do?' she said and shook hands with the smiling pair. 'Many congratulations. I hope you'll be very happy.'

'Welcome—I'm so glad you could come. You must feel you had a hand in all this,' said Sarah warmly, and pressed Olivia's hand. 'I hope Max didn't give you too hard a time before Drew turned up.'

Drew pulled a face, giving Olivia the well-known smile. 'The proverbial bad penny, that's me. Seriously though, Olivia—I may call you Olivia?'

'Of course.'

'I wouldn't have got young Sophie in hot water for the world! She's a honey—young Andrea's a lucky guy.'

'So are you,' returned Olivia. 'By the way, Sophie sends her best wishes to you both——' she halted as the glamorous blonde came tripping up to take Max's arm.

'There you are, *caro*,' she said, tapping his cheek playfully with a beringed hand. 'Where did you lose yourself? I was worried.'

'Allow me to introduce you,' said Max without expression. 'Luisa, this is Mrs Maitland, who I met out in Italy when I was chasing after Drew. Olivia, this is my stepmother.'

The glamorous blonde was Drew's *mother*? Olivia paused for a heartbeat, then held out her hand. 'How do you do?' she said mechanically, trying to conceal her shock.

'How nice to meet you, Mrs Maitland,' said Luisa Hamilton, with a smile that conveyed the exact opposite. 'I am so glad you came—at last.'

'I was so sorry to miss the ceremony,' said Olivia, in total command of herself now. 'My car broke down on the way. I had to wait for someone to come to my rescue.'

'I shouldn't think that was much of a problem!' said Drew, eyeing her in appreciation. 'Surely all you had to do was stand there and look helpless.'

'Unfortunately not,' put in Max. 'Her rescuer was another woman.'

Luisa gave Olivia a look which said plainly that had she herself been in such a predicament men would have swarmed in all directions to help her. 'At least you are here now. *Allora*, tell your best man to introduce Mrs Maitland to some of your guests, Andrea, while I take Max to talk to some old friends.'

'I'll do the introducing myself, Luisa,' said Max with emphasis. 'The old friends can wait. Come and meet Sarah's parents, Olivia.'

'Why,' said Olivia furiously, as he hurried her away, 'didn't you tell me the blonde you were kissing was your stepmother?'

'I had some puerile idea of making you jealous, I suppose,' he said with self disgust, and gave her a black look. 'And it was Luisa who was kissing me, not the other way round.'

'But how *old* is she?' demanded Olivia.

'She was eighteen when my father married her and I was ten. Drew was born a year later.'

'In other words, she's forty-six.'

'And looks younger than me,' said Max sardonically.

'It's blindingly obvious she doesn't look on you as a stepson,' snapped Olivia, so sorry by this time that she'd come near the wedding that she didn't care what she said.

'Do you think I don't know that?' he demanded savagely. 'It's a hellish situation.'

Olivia stopped dead near a group of conifers. 'That's why you wanted me here today, isn't it? As your—your minder, to protect you from Luisa. Or maybe as a sort of cover, to fool people about your true relationship with her.'

'You honestly believe I could even contemplate that kind of thing with her?' Max's eyes blazed with distaste. 'She was my father's wife, for God's sake! She's also Drew's mother! What kind of man do you think I am?'

Olivia looked at him despondently. 'I don't know. I haven't known you long enough to find out. I have no idea what kind of man you are, Max. What I do know is that I don't belong here today. The moment I can decently take my leave I'm going home.'

But first she had to undergo a series of introductions, to the friendly, hospitable couple who were Sarah's parents, and then a series of people Olivia smiled at and responded to with faultless courtesy, until her face was stiff from trying to keep a smile on it. The wedding breakfast proceeded without a hitch, with delicious food served at the tables on the terrace, champagne in abundance, and speeches which varied from sentimental from the bride's father, to wittily jubilant from the bridegroom, and the frankly racy from the best man. And through it all Max sat close at Olivia's side, and Luisa watched them like a hawk. Olivia felt limp with relief when the bridal pair finally departed, with a string of tin cans trailing from Drew's Aston Martin.

'I'll go now,' she said to Max.

'Not before we've had a talk,' he said from the corner of his mouth, waving a hand at a passing friend.

'It's not the time or the place. I must find Sarah's mother to say goodbye, then I'm off.'

'You are leaving so soon?' said a husky voice, and Olivia turned to find Luisa regarding her with un-concealed pleasure. 'What a shame.' She heaved a sigh which showed off her enviable bosom. 'Such a thing to lose my only son.' Her eyes slanted a smile at Max, who stood in poker-faced silence. 'It is so good I have you to comfort me in my loss, *caro*.'

'Drew's married, not dead,' said Max irritably, and took Olivia by the arm. 'Excuse us, Luisa. Olivia wants to say her goodbyes to the Mortimers.'

Olivia detached herself gently, and held out her hand to Luisa. 'Goodbye, Mrs Hamilton. It was a beautiful wedding. You must be very happy for your son.'

Luisa took the hand briefly, her mouth drooping at the corners. '*Naturalmente*. Sarah is a very sweet girl. I hope she will be a good wife for him.'

'More to the point, will Drew be a good husband?' said Max sardonically. 'Don't look so sad, Luisa. Think how much you'll enjoy being a grandmother!'

Luisa's magnificent eyes flashed. 'But not yet, I hope. Sarah is so young to be a mother.'

'What she means,' said Max grimly, as they made their way towards Sarah's parents, 'is that Luisa feels she's too young to be a grandmother.'

'She certainly looks it,' said Olivia coolly. 'Why are you so cold towards her?'

'I just don't like her,' he said with controlled violence.

'You're not indifferent to her, though!'

'What is all this?' Max glared at her. 'What the hell has Luisa to do with you and me?'

'Nothing to do with me, certainly,' said Olivia coldly, then summoned a smile as they joined Sarah's parents. The Mortimers were a friendly couple, who teased Max for letting Drew steal a march on him by getting married first. He slid an arm around Olivia's waist and told them it was something he intended putting right at the first opportunity.

She stiffened, but somehow kept the smile pinned to her face, even when Luisa joined the group and said Olivia must not leave without viewing the beautiful array of wedding presents.

Olivia had sent a pair of George IV silver serving spoons in advance, and wanted to get away more than inspect the other presents, but she couldn't bring herself to refuse. Max, his attention demanded by a brace of bridesmaids, was too late to prevent her being whisked off into the house by the determined Luisa.

'Are they not lucky?' the latter demanded, as they looked at the array of silver and china laid out in the Mortimers' dining room. She turned on Olivia suddenly. 'Are you in love with Max?'

Olivia gave the other woman a faint, composed smile. 'We hardly know each other.'

'It takes no time to fall in love, *cara*,' said Luisa, eyeing Olivia up and down. 'You are very beautiful. But with such cold green eyes. I am surprised. Max, he goes for warmer women usually.'

'How interesting,' said Olivia lightly.

'He is a wonderful lover,' announced Luisa, eyeing her closely.

Olivia blessed her opaque creamy skin which hid the sudden heat in her face. 'I wouldn't know,' she said distantly, trying to ignore the implication in Luisa's statement. But the other woman wouldn't let her.

'You are wondering how *I* know.' Luisa Hamilton smiled like a cat who'd stolen the cream. 'Believe me, I *know*, Mrs Maitland. When he grew so big and strong I never think of him as *figliastro*—stepson, you understand. After my husband die I was lonely, Drew was away at school, but Max—he was there. And he comfort me, as only he know how.'

Olivia'd had enough. 'Now you've done what you came here to do, I must go, Mrs Hamilton.' She smiled coolly. 'It was so interesting to meet you. Goodbye.'

Conscious of Luisa Hamilton's satisfied smile, Olivia walked through the hall blindly, almost blundering into Max.

'Where've you been?' he demanded.

She smiled brightly. 'Powdering my nose. Will you drive me back to my car now, please?'

'I need to talk to you first,' he said urgently.

'If you don't drive me I can always walk,' she went on, as though he hadn't spoken. 'I must get home.'

'I'll follow you,' he said at once, opening the car door for her. 'What's your father's address?'

Olivia knew it was pointless to withhold something Max could easily find out for himself. She provided the necessary details, then gave him a beseeching look.

'Could we leave it until tomorrow, please? I'm very tired, and you must be needed here to see people off and so on. You can pick me up tomorrow afternoon.'

He frowned as he started the car. 'I thought we'd have dinner tonight, sort out whatever's troubling you.'

'I'd rather not, if you don't mind.' She swallowed on a rush of nausea. 'I think I may have eaten something which disagreed with me. I don't feel very wonderful.'

Max shot her a sidelong look of concern as he drove. 'You're as white as a sheet. What the hell's happened to you since I spoke to you last night?'

Olivia, all her concentration needed to stop throwing up in his car, made no response. When Max drew up near the church, she almost shot from the car in her eagerness to get away.

Max sprinted after her as she ran for her father's car. 'Olivia! What the hell's the matter? You can't drive in that state!'

She tossed her hat into the back seat and got behind the wheel. 'I'll be fine. Go back to your guests.' She slammed the door shut and started the car, forcing him to leap away, his face like thunder as she drove off down the road as though all the demons in hell were chasing her.

CHAPTER TEN

OLIVIA drove home to her father's house at breakneck speed and told him she was leaving for London straight away. She explained, shivering, that she'd made a bad mistake where Max was concerned and scribbled a short note, asking her father to give it to Max when he called for her the following afternoon. Deeply grateful for her father's worried forbearance, she collected her belongings, then asked him to take her to the station.

'My note will explain everything to Max,' she assured him as he drove her into Cheltenham. 'If he rings this evening, tell him I'm in bed with a headache.'

'I don't like telling lies for you, Olivia,' said Henry Collins sternly.

She gave a sound somewhere between a sob and a laugh. 'It isn't really a lie, Dad. I've already got the headache, and the minute I get to a certain quiet little hotel I know I'm going to bed.'

'I wish you'd tell me what was wrong.'

'I can't. It involves someone else—and believe me you wouldn't want to know.'

When she arrived at Ealing Broadway Olivia took a taxi to her flat, packed a bag at top speed, then drove herself to a small private hotel and booked a room for a week, rang her father to say she was safe and that she'd report in every day. If he wanted to contact her urgently he could do so at the travel agency. She put her things away in the comfortable, anonymous little room then made herself some tea from the tray provided, but the liquid acted like an emetic on her already queasy stomach, and she rushed into the bathroom to part with the small amount of wedding breakfast she'd managed to eat. Afterwards she lay on the bed like a marble effigy, staring at the blank television, unable to summon the energy to turn it on. It would have been useless anyway, she thought drearily. No programme would have been gripping enough to banish the images of Max and Luisa together. At the thought of it jealousy seared her like a branding iron, and she flopped over on her stomach, burying her head in the pillow in a vain effort to blot the pictures from her mind.

After a sleepless night Olivia forced herself to eat a little breakfast next morning, then went out to buy some Sunday papers, and a couple of paperback novels to while away the time until she could get to work next day. By the evening of what seemed like the longest day of her life she was bitterly regretting her flight from the flat. What an idiot she was, she thought scornfully. Even if Max had come chasing after her—and there was no guarantee that he would have done—she could simply have refused to let him in. But somehow it was difficult to imagine keeping Max out if he'd wanted in. The other tenants in the house might even have called the police if he'd caused a disturbance. Or you'd have let him in to avoid it, she told herself cynically.

Olivia rang her father midway through the evening, to find that Max had not called for her that afternoon. He'd come after her the night before instead.

'Oh, no!' said Olivia wearily. 'Sorry to put you through all that, Dad.'

'I wasn't subjected to anything untoward. The man was remarkably courteous in the circumstances, since it was obvious the contents of the note gave him no pleasure—as I assume you intended?'

'You assume right. Did he stay long?'

'No. He went off in a tremendous hurry to drive to London immediately to see you.'

'You didn't say where I was!' she said in alarm.

'How could I? You didn't trust me with the name of your hotel!' he pointed out.

'Only because I know you hate to lie. Thanks, Dad. Sorry to involve you.'

'I'm your father, Olivia. I expect to be involved, whatever you do.' He paused for a moment. 'If it's of any interest to you, darling, Max Hamilton made a very good impression on me. I liked him.'

Monday was a very tiring day. It was no busier than usual, but rendered hideous for Olivia by the possibility of seeing Max Hamilton striding to her desk to confront her at any minute. When she finished for the day a little after seven, she was conscious of an odd, mortifying feeling of anticlimax. Once she was back at the hotel and in no danger of seeing Max she relaxed a little, took a shower and changed into a thin green cotton dress, then went out to buy some sandwiches to eat in the park near the hotel, reluctant to shut herself up in her room while the sun still shone. From a park bench she watched couples stroll by, some of them laughing together, others so lost in the wonder of their own company Olivia immersed herself in a copy of the *Evening Standard* to avoid seeing them.

The evening established a pattern she kept to for the entire week. But by the end of it Max had neither put in an appearance, nor tried to ring her at her desk, which he could have done, quite easily, she thought, with illogical resentment. She realised now that she'd been cockily certain he'd come chasing after her. If he hadn't told her father he was following her to London she would have taken it for granted her note had finished things between them. Perhaps it had, she thought miserably. He might have changed his mind after leaving her father.

Most ironic of all, she found, as time passed, was that the things Luisa said didn't matter any more. If Max had been tempted to make love to his stepmother at some point in the past it was obvious that he no longer had the slightest desire to do so. And after a long, intolerably empty week without Max one thing Luisa'd said had been the absolute truth. It took no time at all to fall in love. In the brief time she'd known him, Max Hamilton had changed her life so completely that Olivia was depressingly sure it would take the rest of it to get over him, even if she never saw him again.

By the end of a second week Olivia faced facts. Max obviously had no intention of seeking her out again. Pocketing her pride, she dialled the number of his flat, but there was no answer, and no answering machine to take a message. Nor was her luck any better on several subsequent occasions. In the end she gave up, certain Max had changed his mind about staying in the UK and gone abroad again.

On the Friday evening, Olivia had just finished the paperwork for a holiday booked by a couple eager to sample the delights of the new Italian itinerary when she looked up to see a tall, familiar figure, and her heart contracted.

'Hello, Mrs Maitland,' said Drew Hamilton, the celebrated smile conspicuous by its absence.

'Why—hello!' She pulled herself together and held out her hand. 'How do you do? How was the honeymoon?'

'Perfect,' he said succinctly. 'Could we possibly get out of here for a few minutes?'

Olivia nodded. 'I was just about to leave, anyway. I generally walk home at this time of the year. Do you want to walk with me?'

He shook his head. 'The car's parked nearby. I'll drive you.'

The short drive was accomplished in tense silence Olivia couldn't find a way to break for the life of her.

'Would you care to come in?' she asked warily, when he stopped the car.

'Thank you, no. I must get back as soon as possible,' he said brusquely.

Olivia stiffened. Max had obviously been complaining about her treatment, she thought scornfully. Which was surprising. She found it hard to believe that Max had taken his brother into his confidence.

'Are you returning to Birmingham tonight?' she said, for something to say, since Drew was still maintaining a hostile silence.

'No. To Horsleigh, to Sarah's parents. I've left her there for the time being.'

Olivia looked at him questioningly. 'You must have sought me out for a reason. Would you mind telling me what it is?'

'First of all, though it's absolutely no business of mine,' he began, 'would you mind telling me how you feel about my brother?'

'I most certainly would.' Chin raised, she turned her head to look out of the window.

Drew sighed. 'Look, I'm not asking out of idle curiosity, Olivia. It's important that I know, just the same.'

'Why? Did Max send you to ask?'

He looked shocked. 'Good grief, no! Max has no idea I'm here, believe me. To be honest I didn't want to come myself, but Sarah insisted.'

Olivia frowned. 'I don't understand.'

Drew flushed, looking suddenly boyish, and nothing like the confident young television presenter known to millions of viewers. 'Sarah thinks you care for Max, that something happened that day that put a spanner in the works between you two.' He shrugged. 'Oh, what the hell! You must know he went chasing after you to your father's place the evening of the wedding. On the way back he had an accident in the car——' He put a hand on hers swiftly. 'Oh, my God—Olivia! Don't faint on me. He's all *right*. He wasn't killed.'

Olivia pulled herself together. 'What happened?' she demanded hoarsely, her eyes dark in her paper-white face.

'Some idiot shot through a traffic light and went into him—look, Olivia, let me take you inside. You need a drink or something.'

'I need something,' she agreed shakily, glad of his helping hand as she got out of the Aston Martin on legs which wobbled alarmingly. Drew literally hauled her up the stairs to her flat, letting out a sigh of relief when they were inside and Olivia was safely stowed on her sofa.

'Got any brandy?' demanded Drew.

She shook her head impatiently. 'Never mind that, tell me what happened to Max. *Please*! Was he injured; is he in hospital——?'

'He was damn lucky,' said Drew, sitting down beside her. 'He was taken to Gloucester Royal with concussion, a couple of broken teeth, a broken nose, multiple bruising and a sprained ankle.' He smiled at her rather more warmly. 'He's with Sarah's people at the moment. She's nursing him, brave girl—he's a bloody difficult patient.'

Olivia smiled faintly. 'I can imagine. I haven't known your brother long, but I know patience isn't his strongest point.'

'You can say that again,' said Drew with feeling, then took her hand in his gently. 'Sorry to give you a shock. But at least it answered my first question very comprehensively. You really love Max, don't you?'

Olivia nodded dumbly, and he squeezed her fingers.

'Sarah's convinced it's his mental state that's retarding his recovery. I tried ringing your flat but no luck. I even got in touch with your father, but he said he wasn't at liberty to disclose your whereabouts, or words to that effect.'

'Did you tell him about Max's accident?' she asked, astonished.

'No,' said Drew, pulling a face. 'Max made me swear not to. But I was coming to town today anyway, so Sarah made me come along and see you.' He grinned. 'Your father felt able to tell me where you worked.'

Olivia smiled shakily. 'I never thought to swear him to silence about the agency.'

'Lucky for me!' Drew leaned towards her urgently. 'Please come and see Max, Olivia. I mean, he won't die or anything if you don't. But I've never seen him like this before. What the hell happened between you two?'

Unable to mention jealousy of Drew's own mother as the root cause, Olivia shook her head firmly. 'I can't tell you that. By the way, isn't your mother helping take care of Max?'

Drew grinned. 'Lord, no. I adore my mother, but even I admit she's no ministering angel. She went to see Max in hospital, of course, but he wasn't quite himself, to say the least, at first. From the concussion,' he added. 'And they never get on very well, anyway, those two. He wasn't a pretty sight, either. My glamorous Mamma couldn't cope with a snarling invalid who looked like an extra in a horror film. So she flew back to Sacile.'

'I see,' said Olivia, seeing far more than Drew imagined. 'So Sarah's left holding the baby.'

'And a pretty unmanageable baby he is, too!' Drew hesitated. 'You'd be doing us all a great favour, Sarah most of all, if you came back with me now. Will you, Olivia?'

She looked at him for a moment or two, then shrugged. 'Put like that, how can I refuse?' she said at last. 'But you'll have to drive me to my father's house afterwards.'

Drew's face cleared. 'Brilliant! Sarah said you would.'

'Percipient girl!' Olivia smiled. 'Lucky man, aren't you?'

He nodded his fair head fervently. 'Lord knows what a girl like her sees in me, but I never stop thanking my lucky stars she agreed to marry me.' He smiled, and jumped to his feet, holding out a hand to help Olivia up. 'I don't suppose you could give me a sandwich or something before we start? I'm starving.'

Olivia made them a pot of coffee to drink while she threw together some sandwiches they could eat on the way, then took another few minutes to ring her father, and throw clothes into a holdall yet again, so that even with the Aston Martin eating up the miles it was late by the time they arrived in Horsleigh. Lights from the Mortimer house gleamed through the warm, summer dusk as Drew helped Olivia out of the car and took her hand to take her towards the house. He squeezed her fingers encouragingly, sensing her reluctance now she was actually here and about to see Max. Before they could ring the bell, the door opened and Sarah Hamilton threw herself joyfully into her husband's arms, returning his kiss with such interest that it was several seconds before they drew apart.

'I'm sorry, Olivia,' she said, stretching out her hand in welcome. 'I was getting anxious.'

'We got here as fast as we could, sweetheart,' said Drew, keeping an arm round her.

'That was partly what made me anxious!' she said drily. 'Thank you for coming, Olivia—I really appreciate it. Max needs something drastic to lift him out of the black hole he's living in.'

'Is he recovering?' asked Olivia, as Sarah took her to see her parents.

'Physically, yes. Otherwise no. Which is why I sent Drew to find you.'

Olivia stopped in her tracks, her troubled eyes meeting Sarah's. 'He may not want to see me.'

'Don't you believe it!' Sarah smiled mischievously. 'When he was concussed he muttered in his sleep all the time, most of it pretty incoherent, except for your name. That came through loud and clear, according to the hospital staff. They thought you were his wife.'

Only partially reassured, Olivia went to see the elder Mortimers, who gave her a warm welcome, then Mrs Mortimer hurried off to see to a meal for the new arrivals and Drew took Sarah upstairs, directing her to a door at the end of the upper hallway.

'That leads to a sort of self-contained annexe Ted Mortimer had converted from an old barn. Kitty turned it over to Max when he came out of hospital. He's not long gone up, apparently—said he was tired, but I think he just can't stand company for too long at a time.'

'Right.' Olivia squared her shoulders. 'I'll go and get this over with then.'

'You're not facing a firing squad!'

She smiled wryly. 'That's the way it feels.'

She walked quickly towards the door of the guest-room, knocked on it, and without waiting for a reply went inside the room and closed the door behind her.

Max wasn't in bed as she'd expected, but watching a television newscast from a chair, his back turned to her. At his elbow there was a small table with several novels, a bowl of fruit, and a whisky decanter with a half-full glass beside it.

'Sarah?' he said without turning round. 'For God's sake go to bed. I shan't need anything more tonight.'

Olivia, her heart banging against her ribs, walked slowly towards him, and suddenly his head went up and he turned sharply, wincing at a twinge of pain. His eyes met hers incredulously, light leaping in them before his lids came down to snuff all expression from his haggard face.

'What the hell are you doing here?' he said coldly.

'Drew brought me,' she said, swallowing. She hadn't expected arms open in glad welcome, but the cold hostility on Max's face was intimidating. 'He ran into me today in London and told me about—about your accident.'

'Since it was more than a fortnight ago,' he said bitingly, 'I'm practically recovered.'

Olivia eyed him closely. The fading remains of a black eye gave Max a strangely sinister air, but apart from a new dent at the bridge of his nose, and the walking stick leaning against his chair there were no outward signs of his accident.

'Is the concussion better?' she asked, hovering halfway to the door, poised for escape.

'If you mean am I in full control of my faculties, then yes, I'm back to normal.'

'You were lucky.'

His smile sent shivers down her spine. 'Remarkably so. I had a very fortunate escape.'

Olivia took that in the way it was intended. 'From me as well, you mean.'

He shrugged.

The silence between them spun out, lacerating Olivia's nerves. 'Right,' she said at last. 'Now I've seen you and know you're all in one piece I'd better go. Goodbye, Max.'

'Wait!' he said harshly.

'What for?'

'Why did you come?'

'Sarah seemed to think you wanted me to.'

'Sarah takes too damn much on herself sometimes,' he said savagely.

'And why she bothers, I don't know,' retorted Olivia, suddenly furious. 'How ungrateful can you get? The girl's not long back from her honeymoon, insists on staying here to nurse you, worrying herself sick because you're not recovering faster—and all you can do is complain!' She turned on her heel.

'Where are you going?' he rapped out.

'To tell Sarah to get on with her own life and leave you to sort yours out for yourself, you self-centred pig——'

A crack of unwilling laughter halted her in her tracks. She turned, to see Max grinning reluctantly. 'I'm sorry, Olivia.'

'Apologise to Sarah, not me!'

'That's what I meant,' he agreed suavely. 'Sarah doesn't deserve cracks like that.'

'Whereas I do, I suppose.' Olivia's eyes flashed like green fire. 'I came here tonight purely because Drew and Sarah asked me to.'

'I didn't think it was your idea,' he retorted.

'How could it have been? I didn't know you'd had an accident. I hadn't heard a word, remember, so how was I to know what had happened?' She stared at him defensively.

He hauled himself to his feet, balancing with the aid of his stick. 'How could you hear a word? You ran off and hid somewhere. Not even your father knew where you were. I could have been dead and buried by this time for all you knew!' His eyes narrowed. 'I don't suppose you tried to contact *me* in the interim.'

Olivia opened her mouth to deny it then thought better of it. 'Yes, I did,' she admitted unwillingly. 'I rang you once or twice, then gave up. I assumed you'd gone abroad again after all.'

Max's face softened a fraction. He looked at her in silence for a while, as though he were seeing her clearly for the first time now his anger had dissipated a little. Olivia had trouble in keeping still under the analytical scrutiny, then blinked in surprise as Max said the last thing she expected to hear.

'I liked your father, Olivia.'

She gave him a wry little smile. 'The feeling was apparently mutual. Dad didn't approve of lying to you for me. Though if he said I was in bed with a headache he was telling you the truth, except that it was a hotel bed instead of my own.'

'Why did you hole up in a hotel, for God's sake? Even if I'd managed to come after you that night, instead of fetching up in Casualty, all you'd have had to do was tell me to get lost. I wouldn't have hurt you.' Max staggered slightly and Olivia leapt forward to steady him.

'Please sit down,' she begged.

'I will if you will,' he said wearily, and slumped into his chair as she sat on the edge of the bed. 'And don't worry. I'm not concussed any more—it's just this damned ankle.' He fixed her with his good eye. 'So talk, Olivia. Tell me why the maidenly flight.'

'It was something Luisa said,' Olivia told him bluntly.

Max's face set in grim lines. 'I might have known! What did my beautiful stepmother have to say about me? Nothing good, I'm sure.'

'On the contrary. Wonderful was the word she used.'

Max stared at her blankly. 'Are you sure she meant me, not Drew?'

'Oh, yes,' said Olivia with composure. 'She said you were a wonderful lover. How when you grew so big and strong she could no longer look on you as her stepson, and when your father died you became lovers.' Her eyes met his defiantly. 'That's what the lady said.'

'And you believed her!' said Max bitterly.

'She was very convincing. And it's as plain as the nose on your face that she still fancies you even if you no longer want *her*!'

'I never did want Luisa,' he thundered, then closed his eyes, one fist clenched on the arm of his chair. He opened his eyes again, stabbing her with them. 'Obviously you won't believe me until you hear the whole story.'

She shook her head. 'Please—you don't have to——'

'Yes, I do. I know Luisa.' His mouth twisted. 'Lord knows what fairy-story she concocted, but it must have been a good one to send you running off like that.' He stared into space, silent for a moment. 'My father died when I was twenty-two. Drew was away in prep school, and after the funeral he went back there, and I was left with the lamenting widow. The physical side of their marriage had been over for some time, or so Luisa told me. And she was a young, healthy woman about the same age as you are now. I think she loved my father in her own way and felt shaken by his death. It brought her up short, faced with her own mortality, and she felt an urge to celebrate life in the time-honoured way. And I was the nearest, right there in the house. Luisa had never pretended to look on me as a son, nor I on her as a mother. But when she did her best to seduce me I rejected her in no uncertain terms. I was genuinely grieving for my father for one thing. Besides, the thought of his wife in that sense was utterly repugnant to me. Don't get me wrong! Normally I wasn't troubled by puritan tendencies. I was fresh out of college, just starting in my first job, and by no means inexperienced. But the advances of my father's widow sent me running for cover in disgust. And where Luisa's concerned I've been running ever since. Our relationship, at best, has never been more than an uneasy truce.'

Olivia looked at him in silence, knowing beyond all shadow of doubt that she'd just heard the unvarnished truth. 'Luisa was very convincing,' she said quietly at last. 'I'm sorry. For the first time in my life I was burning up with jealousy and——' A shiver ran through her. 'And to be honest the idea smacked of incest. I know there was no blood tie between you, but that didn't prevent me from feeling disgusted.' Her eyes met his in sudden question. 'By why, Max? Why should she say such a thing to me?'

'To get at me, I suppose,' he said morosely. 'She's met other women in my life often enough, but you, it's obvious, made a different impression. Luisa's no dumb blonde. Pure instinct would have told her you were the one woman in the world for me. So by way of revenge for my rejection she told you a lie plausible enough to be taken for the truth.'

'And I believed her,' said Olivia tonelessly. 'I'm sorry, Max.' When he made no effort to answer she glanced at her watch. 'It's late. I must go. I told my father I might be late, but I don't want to worry him too much——' She looked up as a knock on the door heralded Sarah's entrance.

'Mother says Olivia must be hungry,' the new bride said warily. 'And Drew's very tired. Could you bring yourself to stay the night here, Olivia? It would save him a forty-mile round trip.'

Clever Sarah, thought Olivia drily. Put like that, it was a suggestion she'd be churlish to refuse.

'Sensible idea,' said Max firmly, before she could reply. 'Tell your mother Olivia's staying, Sarah.'

Irked by his high-handedness, Olivia would have liked to object, but she curbed her tongue, and confessed that a sandwich on the way had been her only food since breakfast.

'No wonder you look like a ghost!' snapped Max, and smiled suddenly at Sarah, the transformation startling his young sister-in-law as much as Olivia. 'Tell you what—ask your mother if Olivia could have her supper up here on a tray with me. I might even share some of it with her.'

A jubilant Sarah assured him this would be no trouble at all and literally danced from the room, leaving an odd silence behind her.

'I need to ring my father,' said Olivia awkwardly.

Max pointed to the extension beside the bed. 'No problem.'

Feeling awkward under the eyes trained on her face, Olivia dialled her father's number, explained the change of plan as briefly as possible, listened for a moment, promised to ring her father next day and put the phone down.

'Was he surprised?' asked Max.

'Yes. He sends his best wishes for a speedy recovery,' she said stiltedly.

Max's lips twitched. 'That's nice.' He held out his hand. 'Come here.'

Olivia looked at the hand, then shook her head. 'I'll stay here, if you don't mind.'

'I do mind,' he said, and got to his feet awkwardly. 'Ah well, if Mahomet won't come to the mountain…' He limped towards her, leaning on his stick, then lost his footing, and Olivia gave a shriek and sprang forward to catch his fall.

Since Max was a foot taller and built on heroic scale the result was disastrous. They collapsed together in an undignified heap on the floor, the breath squashed out of Olivia as Max landed square on top of her. She tried desperately to get free, terrified Max had injured himself further, but he laughed breathlessly, and pinned her down, his face inches from hers.

'Now I've got you where I want you at last,' he panted, 'it seems too good an opportunity to waste.'

When his mouth met hers Olivia abandoned all thought of struggling, or of anything else. Oblivious to the fact that any one of the other members of the household might come in at any moment, she surrendered to Max's kiss with a stifled sob, her arms freeing themselves only to reach round him as far as she could and clutch him close. Her mouth parted in passionate response to the kiss that did more to heal the breach between them than all the words in the *Oxford English Dictionary*. They were so lost in each other neither noticed the door open, or the startled face of Kitty

Mortimer above a loaded tray, or the fact that the door closed softly again, leaving them to travel the quickest route to conciliation known to man and woman.

A cheerful rat-tat-tat on the door, minutes later, preceded the entry of Drew and Sarah, the former now the bearer of the supper tray.

'Do you need help getting yourself up, Max?' Drew enquired cheerfully. 'Or shall we take this tray away—again—and leave you to it for a bit?'

'Again?' cried Olivia, in an agony of embarrassment.

'That's right. You just shocked my mother-in-law rigid,' he assured her, grinning.

Olivia groaned with embarrassment. 'For heaven's sake let me up, Max.'

'I would if I could,' he said, wincing. 'But at the moment, in my present state of infirmity, it's a bit difficult.'

'Right,' said Drew. 'Sarah, you take hold of one arm and I'll take the other. Right. On the count of three, heave! Good grief, Max, you weigh about a ton more than I thought, considering there's no excess flab on you anywhere.'

'Stop talking and hand me my stick,' panted Max, laughing as he saw the state of Olivia as Sarah helped her to her feet. 'I tripped and fell on her. Are you all right, darling?'

'As well as can be expected,' she said, giggling. 'I feel as if I've been run over by a bus.'

Sarah gave her an impulsive hug. 'I've never seen you laugh before. At the wedding you had such a cool little smile on your face all the time. I thought Max had fallen for an iceberg.'

'Didn't look like an iceberg to me just now,' said Drew in mock-disapproval. 'Rolling round on the floor like that. Tut-tut, Mrs Maitland.'

'Don't call her that,' ordered Max, sinking into the chair. 'As soon as I can argue her into it she'll be Mrs Hamilton.'

'Why the argument? Don't you want to marry Max?' asked Sarah, handing Olivia a plate of chicken salad.

Olivia laughed helplessly. 'I seem to be coming round to the idea slowly.'

'Well, hurry it up a bit,' ordered Drew. 'Any more of Max's bear-with-a-sore-head act and we'll all go bananas.'

'I did have a sore head,' Max pointed out, attacking his supper with enthusiasm.

'I thought you'd had dinner,' said Drew, surprised.

'He hasn't eaten a proper meal since the accident, according to Mother,' Sarah informed him, and smiled at Olivia. 'I knew he'd be all right once he saw you again.'

'I hope you are going to marry me, Olivia,' said Max, fixing her with a commanding eye. 'Think of the blow to my ego if you turn me down after the lengths these two have gone to.'

'Why weren't you keen to marry him?' asked Drew bluntly.

'Not that it's any business of yours,' said Max with emphasis, 'but it may have escaped your notice that Olivia's been married before. The experience didn't endear her to the thought of repeating it—even with a prize catch like me,' he added modestly.

'Will you all stop discussing me as if I didn't have a tongue in my head?' said Olivia, laughing in spite of her embarrassment. 'I give in—if only to get you to change the subject.'

But Max wasn't laughing. 'Did you mean that?' he asked sternly.

She nodded, her eyes luminous as they met his, and very quietly Sarah took Drew by the hand and pulled him from the room.

'Take this plate, Olivia,' ordered Max, and, all inclination to argue about anything at all having deserted her, she did as she said, put their plates on the tray on the table beside him, then helped him to his feet.

'Where do you want to go now?' she asked breathlessly, supporting him.

'To bed,' he said briefly. 'Don't panic. I just want to rest this blasted ankle, and hold you in my arms in comfort for a while, during which time I'll give you a hundred and one good reasons for your wisdom in saying yes, at last.'

'I wasn't refusing to—er—co-habit with you before,' she pointed out, as they sank on the bed together.

'After you ran away from the wedding I thought you'd changed your mind, permanently,' he said grimly.

Olivia pulled his head down to hers and kissed him lingeringly. 'Only for a while, until I got over Luisa's little revelation. After a few days without you I found I didn't care whether you'd once made love to her or not. The only important thing in life was to make sure you restrict your activities to me in the future.'

Max crushed her to him in response to this gratifying statement. 'I love you, Olivia. I never knew how much until it seemed I'd lost you.'

'Likewise,' she assured him, rubbing her cheek against his. 'One thing Luisa was utterly right about— it takes no time to fall in love.'

'I never thought I'd agree with her about any-thing,' he said, chuckling. 'But she's dead right about that. One look—well, no,' he added scrupulously, 'two looks at you was all it took.'

'Ah, but will you feel the same twenty years from now?'

'For the rest of my life,' he assured her emphati-cally, then told her to look in the zipped pocket of the suitcase on the chest at the end of the bed.

Olivia did as he said, holding up a small box. 'Is this what you wanted?'

Max nodded. He heaved himself upright and held out his arms. Olivia ran to him and sat on the edge of the bed in his embrace. 'Open the box,' he ordered.

'Don't you ever say please?' she scolded, then gasped as she discovered a pair of emerald earrings gleaming from a bed of satin. 'Oh, Max!'

'The correct stake for our bet, if I remember cor-rectly,' he said, kissing her.

'But I thought I got those if I won,' she said when she could speak.

'Does it matter who won, darling, as long as no one lost?' he said huskily, and drew her down on the bed into his arms. 'Not,' he said in the second before their lips met, 'that the stones shine nearly as bright as your eyes, my beautiful girl.'

'That's the tears,' she said thickly, rubbing her face against his. 'Oh, Max, I've been so unhappy!'

'Never again!' he assured her, and began showing her very graphically just how happy he intended to make her from that moment on.

It was some time before she could tear herself away. 'Where are you going now?' he demanded.

'This may be the happiest night of my life,' she said wryly, 'but I'm not so lost to the refinements that I can keep my hostess on tenterhooks wondering if I need another bed or not, which I most certainly do. Since we're going to be married after all, we might as well get in the *Guinness Book of Records* as the only couple of such advanced years to wait for the privilege until their wedding-night!'

When Olivia and Max Hamilton arrived in Asolo for their honeymoon on a perfect evening a few weeks later the moon was at the full, and their room looked just as inviting as the first time Olivia had slept there, but with one difference. A vast bed with a carved headboard replaced the two smaller ones of her previous visit.

She stared at it in awe as Max sent the porter away with a lavish tip. He took her in his arms, grinning.

'I know you wanted the same room, but after waiting this long to share it with you I'm damned if I was going to put up with twin beds!'

'You actually rang up and ordered a double bed?' she said, giggling.

'You bet I did. I specified one suitable for my dimensions while I was at it, too,' he assured her and kissed her lightly, showing her, she knew perfectly well, that this was to be a wedding-night so different from her first experience no shadows from the past would be allowed to spoil it.

'Come on,' he said briskly. 'Ten minutes to unpack, ten minutes to shower and change, then downstairs to dinner.'

In the rush to keep to this itinerary there was a lot of jostling and laughing horseplay before Olivia rushed to take her shower, so happy that she sang at the top of her voice among the flower-painted tiles as she stood under the warm spray. She swathed one of the enormous white towels around her sarong-fashion, then raced from the bathroom to collide with her husband, who was just raising his hand to knock on the door. The impact sent the towel to the floor and Max dived to retrieve it, then straightened, arrested, as Olivia stood suddenly still, making no effort to cover herself. She smiled slowly, her eyes rivalling the emeralds in her ears against the delicate flush which receded slowly, his eyes following it in fascination as it retreated down her throat and lost itself in the valley between her breasts. His gaze moved lower, taking in every curve and hollow of her motionless body, his eyes lingering in almost tactile caresses at certain points of interest, and her breasts rose and fell more rapidly, and his eyes dilated and his jaw clenched. Then his arms reached out and she moved, closing the space between them as she raised brilliant, inviting eyes to his.

'Do we have to go down to dinner?'

Max swung her up in his arms. 'No. Dinner can come to us—later.'

'Much later,' she agreed, pulling him down to her as he laid her on the flagrantly inviting bed.

Max laughed deep in his throat, kissing and caressing her and removing his clothes at the same time, a skill she must remember to tease him about, she thought hazily, as all the excitement and joy of the day rose up inside her in a tide of love which swept away everything other than the joy of being here at

the right time and the right place and in the arms of
the one man in the world she wanted to spend the rest
of her life with.

Max was in no hurry. His lips followed his hands
on a path which moved over every inch of her body,
lingering so long over the process that every last one
of Olivia's nerves was tuned to such concert pitch that
she instituted a counter attack of her own, caressing
her husband's broad muscular shoulders with urgent
fingers, smoothing her hands over the spare waist and
down his spine, finding, at last, the hard, pulsing
proof of his need. He gave a smothered sound,
breathing in great, ragged gasps as he lost the control
he'd been exerting over himself. He swept his hands
up her yielding body to caress her breasts, teasing the
nipples until they stood proud and wanton, and she
stifled a little shriek as his mouth closed over one of
them, his teeth grazing the sensitised tips as he held
her cruelly tight with one arm, his free hand moving
lower to part her legs, giving his long fingers access
to the hot, hidden place which throbbed in wanton
response to his caresses. Olivia arched her back wildly,
thrusting her hips against him, and Max slid his hands
to cup her bottom, and entered her suddenly, joining
them together with a jolt of such pure physical ec-
stasy that it took their breath away for a moment as
they clutched each other close in a tangle of arms and
legs as their mouths met and the tongues caressed each
other, and their bodies moved convulsively in a relentless, delirious rhythm which brought them so
rapidly to mutual culmination that Olivia made a
protesting murmur in Max's arms as the throbbing
spasms died away.

'I didn't want it to end,' she said huskily against his chest, and felt him shake with amusement against her. He raised her face, smiling victoriously into her tearwet eyes.

'That disposes of the usual question, anyway.'

She scowled at him. 'Usual, indeed! What do you mean?'

'It's customary to ask "how was it for you?"'

'I must have been perfectly obvious how it was for me!' she said tartly, and smiled, stretching against him luxuriously. 'What a waste,' she said, sighing.

Max frowned. He put a fingertip under her chin to raise her face to his. 'Waste?'

'All those years we didn't know each other.'

His face softened. 'We'll make up for it, my darling, I promise you.' He laughed suddenly as her stomach gave a very unromantic rumble. 'I'll order supper. What shall we have—apart from champagne?'

'Something strengthening,' she said demurely, sliding from the bed.

He charged across the bed in a rugby tackle, capturing her in his arms. 'You may regret you said that,' he threatened, and kissed her until she begged for mercy.

They ordered a light, extravagant supper, standing at the windows in each other's arms admiring the moonlight on the garden below while they waited for it. Afterwards, over the meal, they went over the wedding in every detail, Olivia so happy with her day she wanted to relive every minute of it while it was still fresh in her mind.

'Not that I'm likely to forget any of it, ever,' she declared as she raised her glass to him. 'To you, darling. For making it all so perfect for me.'

He shook his head, his dark eyes utterly serious. 'You were the one who made it perfect, Olivia. When I turned at the altar steps and saw you coming towards me in that stunning white dress I almost asked Drew to pinch me to see if I was awake.'

Max had touched Olivia deeply by insisting on a traditional white wedding-dress, brushing aside her half-hearted protests, and in the end she'd delighted her husband, and everyone who laid eyes on her, in an ivory chiffon dress with a dark green sash, a spray of rosebuds and ivy in her hair to echo the sheaf of roses and trailing ivy she carried.

'I read somewhere that girls in Ancient Rome wore a green girdle to their weddings, so as we met in Italy and I remembered what you told me about the colour of Venus, I thought it would be a nice little touch,' she said happily. 'And Sophie and Sarah looked gorgeous in that subtle dark green.'

'I wasn't looking at them,' said Max, sliding an arm round her. 'In the words of the song, my beautiful wife, I only had eyes for you.' He kissed her lightly, then kissed her again, his lips parting hers with sudden urgency. He drew back, looking deep in her eyes as he drew an unsteady breath. 'If there's nothing more you want,' he said hoarsely, 'I vote we pile all this stuff on the tray and leave it outside the door.'

Olivia jumped up with alacrity, stacking the plates at top speed, giggling as they rattled precariously when Max dumped the tray outside their door. He made sure the door was locked, then came back to sit with her on the sofa, and she curled up against him with an ecstatic sigh.

'I can hardly believe we're finally here, together, like this. Though we didn't make it to the *Guinness Book of Records* after all,' she added gleefully.

Max hugged her close. 'My intentions were of the purest,' he said with mock regret, 'but somehow, once we were officially engaged my good intentions flew out of the window. And you were no help at all, if you remember.'

Olivia looked up at him. 'I've got a confession to make,' she said quietly, suddenly very sober. She felt Max tense. 'It's nothing very terrible,' she assured him quickly, 'but I was glad your defences crumbled in the end.'

His eyes met hers, narrowing in sudden under-standing. 'You mean that, deep down, you still har-boured fears about the end result if we'd waited?'

She nodded. 'Stupid, I know. But this time I wanted to come to my wedding-night knowing that it would be the perfect bliss it's supposed to be. And oh, Max, it is!' She reached up to kiss him. 'So I don't regret anything. It was lovely and unpremeditated the first time, but it wasn't perfect, mainly because I was a bit tense and afraid I'd disappoint you—don't laugh! I was, honestly. But tonight it *was* perfect—utterly. But only because we've made love a few times before and I'm getting better at it every time. From the vantage point of experience I now realise it probably isn't perfect the first time very often for anyone. But you must admit I've learnt very quickly. Of course,' she added, poker-faced, 'not every pupil has such a fan-tastic tutor!'

Max gazed down at her wordlessly for a moment, his hard features softened momentarily by a look of tenderness which brought her up into his arms, to kiss him with such abandon that he would have picked her up and carried her to the bed, but she shook her head.

'There's something I want to do first,' she said.

'Whatever it is, don't take too long about it,' he ordered. 'We've got a lot of time to make up, Mrs Hamilton!'

She smiled provocatively, picked up a small overnight bag and went into the bathroom and closed the door. In a feverish hurry she stripped off her clothes, sprayed herself with perfume, then took out the nightgown bought for the occasion. Cut like the robe of a Greek goddess, leaving one shoulder bare, it was made of sea-green silk chiffon which revealed far more than it concealed. She opened the door very quietly to find Max at the window, looking out at the moonlit landscape.

'Max,' she said softly, and he turned, smiling, then stood still, the smile fading.

'Do you like it?' she asked uncertainly. 'I searched high and low before I found the right colour.'

He walked towards her slowly, his eyes travelling over her with such undisguised pleasure she smiled, reassured. 'The colour of Venus,' he said softly, and picked her up in his arms. 'Only she couldn't possibly have held a candle to my beautiful wife.'

'Is it possible you're prejudiced? Does anyone really know what she looked like?' asked Olivia breathlessly as he laid her on the bed.

Max shrugged as he gazed down at her. 'Botticelli painted Simonetta Vespucchi as Venus rising from the foam. And there's the statue of Venus de Milo——'

'I've got one great advantage over *her*, anyway,' chuckled Olivia. 'I've got arms!'

Max laughed and turned out the lights, then joined her in the depths of the wide bed, to hold her close.

'A pity Luisa had a cold and couldn't come to the wedding,' said Olivia.

Max chuckled. 'For once I think she showed remarkable tact!'

'Shall we go and see her in Sacile?'

'She's in France again. An old flame of hers—a Frenchman, according to Drew—has just gone through a messy divorce. She's comforting him.'

'Good. She's a very beautiful woman. I imagine most men would welcome some comforting from Luisa.'

He chuckled. 'How magnanimous you are!'

'Tonight,' said Olivia expansively, stretching herself against him, 'I feel magnanimous to the entire world.'

'Never mind the world, darling. For tonight just concentrate on me!'

She obeyed him with such fervour the moon slid down the sky and made a graceful exit before they returned to earth again.

'Would you be deeply offended,' said Olivia a long time later, 'if I said I was a bit tired? One way and another I need some sleep.'

Max held her close, fitting her head into the curve of his shoulder. 'We both need some sleep. Which actually does come into the category of first experiences. On the other, very few occasions I've made love to you I always left like a gentleman afterwards and stole away into the night.'

Olivia chuckled sleepily, burrowing her head into his shoulder as she heaved a sigh of satisfaction. 'Will you make a solemn promise to be here from now on when I wake up?'

'I believe the fitting response is one I've made once already today,' he said, kissing her hair. 'As long as we both shall live. Will that do?'

'Perfectly!'